Sapient Salvation Book 1

THE SELECTION

SAPIENT SALVATION BOOK 1

THE SELECTION

JAYNE FAITH
with CHRISTINE CASTLE

Sapient Salvation book one: The Selection
a novel by Jayne Faith with Christine Castle

Paperback Edition ISBN: 978-0-9905639-9-0

Edited by: Tia Silverthorne Bach of Indie Books Gone Wild

Published in the United States of America

Interior design and formatting by E.M. Tippetts Book Designs
www.emtippettsbookdesigns.com

Also by Jayne Faith and Christine Castle

The Seas of Time

The Laws of Attraction

1

Maya

IT WAS A day like any other in that Lana was down below singing and weaving ceremonial rope with her nimble fingers, and I was up in the trees filling collections bags with yellow-orange bergamine fruits. But it wasn't any other day, and my mind wasn't on my work. How could it be? It was the most important day of my nearly twenty years.

The singing below went silent mid-verse. "Maya?" Lana called.

I started and looked around guiltily, realizing I'd stopped picking as I'd let Lana's song and my own thoughts distract me from my duties.

"All's well," I called to my sister, hoping I sounded calm. Not that I expected to fool Lana. She knew me better than I knew myself.

Instead of pressing me about why I'd paused my work, she took up her song again. She didn't have to ask what was on my mind. It was the same thing that was on everyone's mind: the Selection. At dusk, Lana and I would represent our clan by entering the Selection along with the other young men and women of Obligate Elect age.

And after the Selection, everything would be different.

I lifted my bag, checking its heft. I'd already reached the day's quota for myself, but I couldn't stop until I had enough to turn in for Lana, too.

I climbed higher, going for the bergamines in the highest branches where most of the pickers were too afraid to climb. It *was* dangerous—the canopy branches were too long and slender to support a person's weight—but Court and I had figured out how to pull them through and around each other to create stronger boughs to climb on.

We'd even created a suspended platform, a spot where we frequently met. Our nest, Court called it. I didn't really have any spare time, but I longed for a few moments alone with Court before the Selection.

I checked the angle of the sun, and a point low in my core warmed and stirred with anticipation. "I'm going up to the canopy," I called down to Lana. Court would be up there.

I quickly climbed up through the branches, looking for the notches that told me where it was safe to put my hands and feet.

The air up there felt lighter and just more *free* somehow. I breathed deeply, pulling myself up the last few feet. When my head rose over the edge of the nest, I gasped with delight at the sight of Court's smiling face.

He lounged on his side, and my gaze dropped to where the hem of his shirt had pulled up to reveal a stripe of tanned, muscled stomach just above the waistband of his shorts. His blonde hair was darkened with sweat around his temples and his gray-green eyes sparkled when he saw me.

Court was the most gorgeous, perfect man I'd ever known. From the dimple in his left cheek to the warm timbre of his voice to how he caressed my cheek with a gentle touch of his index finger . . .

My pulse raced in anticipation of his hands on my skin. I hung my bergamine collection bags on a stump of a branch that jutted out from the nearest trunk and crawled across the swinging intertwined branches and into Court's arms.

He pulled me against his chest and turned onto his back, and our nest swayed gently. Our lips met, and his hands slid down my sides, over the curve of my lower back, and down to grip my backside. I kissed him more deeply, and he lifted his hips, grinding his arousal into me and bringing a moan to my throat.

"I can hardly wait to have you, to truly make you mine," Court growled. His lips moved to a spot just under my jaw.

"After the Selection, I will be yours forever," I whispered. "And it will be that much sweeter because we waited."

Even though we'd been together for a year and a half, I was still a virgin. We were waiting until we were married. Our hearts were already joined, but I wanted our bodies to couple only after it was safe. After we knew we could be together forever.

His lips trailed down my neck. Then we half rolled so we were on our sides with our chests pressed into one another.

"Mmm . . ." I moaned my pleasure, opening my eyes to look up at the pieces of blue sky peeking through the canopy overhead. In the light of day I couldn't see the fiery battles raging beyond the shield, the invisible bubble that enclosed the Ten Protected Zones of Earthenfell.

"Maya," he said, his lips moving against my throat. "The scent of bergamine blossoms will forever turn me on."

"I need to continue collecting," I murmured, his mention of the fruit blossoms reminding me of my duties. "I don't have enough for Lana's quota yet."

He groaned his dissent and planted one last kiss on my lips.

We never had much time for each other, but each time that we met and brought a few minutes of pleasure into our lives I counted as a victory. It was a victory for the freedom inherent in the love between two people, a victory over the suppression of humans by the alien races that battled for Earthenfell.

Just before I turned to reach for my bergamine bags, something caught my eye. On all fours, I reached out and plucked at Court's climbing shorts and came away with a long, red-orange hair that waved at perfect intervals. With the hair pinched between my thumb and forefinger, I sat back on my heels.

I held the strand up in front of my eyes. My focus switched to Court's face. "What's this?"

He frowned at my hand and then quickly smoothed his face. "Looks like a strand from a Selection ceremony rope. Probably picked it up when I passed Lana and her weaving."

With an impish upturn of one corner of his mouth, Court crawled toward me. He slipped a hand around the back of my neck and drew me into another long kiss, leaving me breathless when he pulled away.

Then he was over the side of the nest and shimmying down the nearest trunk. I slung my collection bags across my body and followed.

The glow of being with Court faded, and I needed to push to get Lana's quota. No time to linger in the groves after the horn. We'd need to get home, bathe, and ready ourselves for the Selection ceremony at dusk.

I moved down, just under the canopy of the spindly topmost boughs, to continue picking.

Far below, Lana had taken up her song again. The sweet sound of her clear voice made its way up to me like a gentle updraft. I wished I could sing so beautifully, but I didn't begrudge her talent. Ever since the fever had taken Lana's sight, Mother reminded us that my sister's voice was the gift she'd received in place of her sight. When I was a child, I'd insisted that the fever had only changed Lana's eyes and that her throat and my throat were still identical. But try as I might, I couldn't produce those lovely sounds. Maybe there was some truth to what Mother said.

My skin glistened with sweat as I worked to fill Lana's collection bags. I got into a rhythm of plucking and climbing, plucking and climbing, methodically moving from tree to tree.

When the horn sounded, I quickly reached for one more bergamine to top off the last bag.

My picking had taken me so far from where Lana sat under a shady tree, with her skeins of colored floss and her dented water canteen, I couldn't even hear her voice.

Back on the ground, I turned to orient myself and then set off in the direction of the setting sun.

At the sound of voices, I paused. When I recognized Court's low laugh, a warm bloom of happiness lifted my heart. On light feet, I headed his direction.

Another voice, a female voice, answered his laugh with a trilling giggle. My shoes scraped to a halt.

As I watched, Farrah emerged from a thick stand of saplings, tugging her shirt down over the ivory skin of her stomach. She giggled again and cast a coquettish look over her shoulder, her waves of red-orange hair swinging as she turned her head.

Waves of red-orange hair . . . The thread on Court's shorts . . . He *wouldn't* . . .

Court came running up behind her. He wrapped his arms

around her waist and buried his face in her hair. She playfully tried to pull out of his grasp, and one of his hands slid up to squeeze her breast. She slapped it away and turned, taking slow backward steps away from him as if trying to entice him to chase her.

My heart iced over. The chill crept outward to freeze my limbs.

"You're insatiable," Farrah said, looking at him from under her eyelashes.

He ran at her again and caught her in his arms, again from behind. Then, he slid a hand down over her shorts between her legs.

She pushed his arm away and turned to face him, pressing her body into his. "Tonight," she said. "Find me after the Selection and fill me again. Twice if you can manage it."

I gasped and slapped a hand over my mouth, pressing against the bile rising up my throat.

At the sound, Court's head jerked around.

Our eyes met, and irritation flashed across his face, followed quickly by dismay.

The heat of anger and humiliation fueled my muscles, melting the freeze of a moment ago in one hot surge. I was off like a shot through the trees, my bags bouncing against my back and hips.

Court followed for a bit, calling after me, but gave up after a minute or so—all too quickly, considering.

When I neared the vicinity of Lana's tree, I stopped and

bent over, my hands planted on my knees. The collection bags slid off my shoulders and bumped to the ground, spilling bergamines.

I retched, but nothing came up.

After a few ragged breaths, I straightened and swiped my fingers across the dampness under my eyes.

I slowly picked up the scattered fruits and tried to focus on collecting myself as well before I walked the last several yards to my sister.

Two thoughts fought like feral cats in my mind. How could Court do such a thing to me? And how could I not have *known*?

Around and around, the two questions clawed at each other, slicing flesh and drawing blood that seemed to stream straight from my heart.

Dazed, I set the collection bags next to the ones I'd left with Lana throughout the day.

"What is it, Maya?" Lana had already wound her skeins in neat bundles. She held the cord she'd been working on all week, woven of the three colors of our clan's seal.

There were no red-orange strands in Lana's skeins. I'd known that. I just hadn't *wanted* to know it.

"Just a bit tired," I said.

I bent to pile her skeins into her weaving case, and she held out the finished cord for me to add.

"I can tell by the way you're breathing that something's wrong."

A faint smile cut through my shock and anger. "I'll tell you about it after the Selection is over."

She lowered her eyelids partway and smiled with a sly stretch of her lips. "No you won't, you'll be too busy celebrating with Court."

I winced.

"Never too busy for you, sister." The sudden pressure of tears swelled around my throat, and I clamped my teeth hard onto my lips.

Damn Court.

I helped her stand and then hooked half of the collection bags over her thin shoulders. I carried her case as well as the rest of the bergamine bags. With her hand on the crook of my elbow, we started toward the drop station.

Lana had no trouble keeping up with me, and there was no hesitation in her steps. She always said that she trusted me to lead her down the safest path, and the way she moved always reminded me of her confidence in my protection. I kept her from tripping over roots. I made sure her quotas were fulfilled so she would receive her full ration. I helped masked the true extent of her debility so she could remain at home with me and Mother.

I didn't resent any of it, not for one second. But I worried. What would become of her if something happened to me?

Someone came up beside me. "How was your day's collection?" Rand's soft but deep voice pulled me from my thoughts.

I managed a smile for him. "It went well, two quotas filled," I said.

He nodded and a chunk of hair the color of strong coffee fell across his forehead. "I have more than I need, but if you don't need them, then today I will turn in a few extra bergamines for the overlords' pleasure."

Rand often picked more than his quota, and nearly every day checked with me and Lana to make sure we had enough. I never wanted to assume he would help me fulfill my and my sister's daily collections, but it was nice to know he was there to help all the same.

I'd seen others try to take advantage of his generosity, lazing or socializing for part of the day and then going to Rand to ask for his surplus. He would always give it once at least to someone who claimed need, but Lana and I were the only ones he offered it to regularly.

"I imagine you're looking forward to the completion of this Selection cycle with great anticipation," he said, tilting his face to look down at me.

I skirted a glance in his direction, but didn't raise my eyes to his. I knew what he was hinting at. That after the Selection, Court and I would finally be married. That's what I'd thought up until I'd seen him grabbing at Farrah, until I'd heard her say—I squeezed my eyes closed, silencing her voice in my head.

"I . . . Um . . . not as much as you might think . . ." I trailed off, unable to fake any enthusiasm.

Lana turned to me, and I could feel the question on her face, poised on the tip of her tongue.

A trilling giggle spilled through the late afternoon heat.

I knew who it was. I should have kept my eyes ahead. But a dozen heated emotions boiled up through me and gathered behind my eyes and around the center of my chest.

I turned.

Farrah was poking at Court's ribs. He was trying to ignore her, but she persisted in touching him, tickling him, bumping against him, preening with her fingers in her wavy hair when he looked her way.

Rand saw, of course.

"Farrah, stop grabbing me," Court hissed, loud enough for the three of us to hear.

Surprise passed over Lana's face, and then disbelief. Anger came last. She'd probably just displayed the exact expressions I had when I'd come upon Court and Farrah in the orchard.

Lana half-turned her head toward me, her eyes flashing. "That *snake*," she spat. Her cheeks flushed.

I nearly smiled in spite of the humiliation that burned on my own face. That Lana could piece together my off mood and one sentence from Court and come up with what was probably close enough to the truth, well, it was a testament to our bond as twins. And even more so it was a tribute to her ability to read people without the benefit of actually seeing their expressions, actions, and body language.

I ground my teeth and fought to keep angry tears from

spilling over. "The worst kind of snake," I said. "The kind of snake who allows his little snake to lead him around."

Out of the corners of my eyes, I flicked a glance up at Rand. His lips were parted and a frown furrowed his brow. I saw the exact moment that the truth clicked. His deep brown eyes widened just a hair, and something lit in them. I knew what it was—hope. But to Rand's credit, he shook his head and shot a look of outrage at Rand and Farrah.

"Maya, I'm sorry." Rand shook his head again. "That man *is* the worst kind of snake. And an utter idiot. He does not deserve you."

I took a shaking breath. My bones felt too fragile, my head too light, and my feet too heavy. But with Lana on my left and Rand on my right, I somehow stayed upright and kept moving one foot in front of the other.

"Thank you," I whispered.

Lana was fuming, waves of anger practically buffeting me like a desert wind. She cursed under her breath, which I'd only heard her do maybe twice ever.

"I'm going to spike his brew with cobalt tonight. Hers too," she said, her voice carrying over the chatter of pickers walking to the drop station.

Several heads swiveled our way.

"Shh," I cautioned.

But it wasn't a half-bad idea. Cobalt was the dye she used for the blue strands of her ceremonial cords. If ingested, it had horrible digestive effects. I wouldn't mind seeing Court and

Farrah sick from both ends for the entirety of the Selection Fete that evening and Feast Day the following day. No, I wouldn't mind that at *all*. In fact, I just might take some of Lana's cobalt and spike their mugs myself.

In my peripheral vision, I saw Court and Farrah slow. They were letting us get ahead so we would have our backs to them in the drop line.

"Maya," Rand said. He cleared his throat. "I imagine that some of your plans for the night have now been, um, spoiled. I hate the thought of that. Tonight, I would be honored if—if you would . . . Will you allow me to escort you to the Fete?"

I let out a big breath and gave him as broad a smile as I could muster. I was in no mood for a party, but I was *not* going to hide away at home while Court was out living it up. "Yes." I nodded firmly. "I would love that."

The look on Rand's face nearly broke my heart. His features seemed to be battling between expressing elation about my answer and sympathy over my predicament.

I knew he'd been in love with me for years. Why hadn't I chosen Rand instead of Court long ago?

Rand was handsome, kind, intelligent . . . and he would *never* betray me the way Court had. It was only beginning to dawn on me how horribly foolish I'd been.

I'd ignored Court's extraneous flirtations, telling myself it didn't matter who he smiled at as long as he kept meeting me in our nest. As long as he kept saying that we'd be married after the Selection.

With a fresh flash of humiliation, I realized how stupid I'd been. Court had never proposed. He'd talked about marriage, yes, but never made the slightest move to secure my hand. I suppose I'd always assumed he would do it after the Selection. That evening. Yes, I'd always been so sure that we would become engaged at the Fete, the rowdy celebration that began as soon as the Selection ceremony ended.

But we'd never made any plans for a life together. We'd never talked about whether we would live in my family's home or his. When we'd petition to have a child. How we'd save for a home of our own.

I pulled my collection bags from my shoulders and began passing them to the man who set them on a scale.

"It's half of my favorite matched set," he greeted me—us, me and Lana.

"Good evening, sir," I said.

When he turned, the spinal implant at the base of his skull caught the light, glinting like a brief wink of a robotic eye.

I watched the scale. Eight bags heavy with bergamines equaled one-eighth of a pound over quota. The man gave a satisfied grunt and entered the weight next to my name with a few taps of his fingers on his tablet. He held out the thin, transparent device so I could sign my name with the tip of my index finger. The tablet flashed green.

Then I moved aside and Lana took my place. She smiled and nodded, but kept her head down as she handed over her collection bags. It was better if she acted shy and avoided trying to make eye contact.

Despite our charade, the man who weighed our bags had to know Lana couldn't see. But we felt it was safer to carry on our act because it enabled him to carry on his act, too. He was an Earthen, but a direct underling of the overlords and could, if he desired, report Lana for her disability. He could report me for helping her hide it.

When it came time for Lana to sign, she held her finger out. The man positioned the tablet under it so that when she lowered her finger to sign it hit the right spot. The tablet flashed green again, and she sidestepped toward me.

I slipped my fingers around her elbow and guided her away while Rand turned in his bags.

"Where are they?" Lana whispered, her eyes flashing.

I cast a glance at the line. "About a dozen back."

"Do you want to wait for Court? I imagine there are more than a few things you'd like to say to him."

"No. I'll speak to him later." I paused, my teeth pulling at my bottom lip for a moment. "And I'll need some of your cobalt."

Lana smirked. "Good girl."

We waited for Rand and then set off toward Southside Borough.

This time of day had always felt bitter as Court and I were forced to part ways. Not anymore. I sent up a prayer of thanks to the stars that Court lived in a different neighborhood.

I stood up as tall as I could and pushed out a long breath,

wishing I could expel Court from my mind and my heart as easily as the air from my lungs. Despite the crushing ache around my heart, Lana and I had a busy night ahead. Preparations for the Selection Ceremony, the Fete for which Rand would be my escort, and some blue-tinged revenge to exact on Court and Farrah.

2

Maya

SLICES OF BERGAMINE and petals from mother's ginger lilies floated around me in our hammered copper soaking tub. It was one of many tubs that had been passed down through the ages for rituals such as the Selection Day cleansing. Across the Ten Protected Zones, many other young men and women were sitting in similar tubs.

I caught a bergamine circle in my palm and lifted it to my nose. My mouth watered at the sweet citrus smell, but the sudden memory of squeezing fruit juice onto Court's lips and then licking it off made my eyes sting. The ache in my chest expanded as I let a few tears fall and mingle with the bath water.

In my self-pity, I almost regretted that I wouldn't be the one from my clan who would go to Calisto and compete for

Lord Toric's favor, just to escape Court and Farrah. But my family and the others in our clan had made the customary tithes to Belinda's parents to pay for her coaching, compensate her family for the loss of their daughter, and provide money in place of her work ration while she trained to compete as our clan's Obligate.

And I knew I should count myself lucky. In some clans, the Obligate was chosen on Selection Day by random drawing. There was no time for preparation and no compensation for the family. I did not understand that approach, as those Obligates rarely fared well in the competition and many of them didn't even survive it. An Obligate entering the competition with no training was walking into almost certain death.

The families of Obligates who perished in the competition never knew exactly how their son or daughter died, and the bodies of the deceased were never returned to Earthenfell. I'd attended a few Obligate funerals, and the mourning families always had the same haunted look in their eyes.

"Maya?" came my mother's voice through the bathroom door. "Five more minutes."

"Yes, mother," I answered, my thoughts returning to the day, to Court.

I sank low in the water, submerging my entire body from the neck down. If only I could hide there forever.

I WATCHED MY reflection in the narrow, full-length mirror

leaning against the wall of my mother's bedroom. The sides of my dark hair were pulled back in gentle swoops, and the ends of my hair curled over my shoulders.

"Arms up."

I obeyed as Mother bent to pull the ceremonial cord around my waist, passing it around three times. She moved around in front of me to secure the rope in a complex knot, leaving the ends to hang down the front of my white ceremonial gown.

The silken cord woven by my sister displayed the colors of our clan: cobalt, aubergine, and sage. All of the clansmen and women between the ages of eighteen and twenty—the Obligate Elects—would wear white garb and clan cords for the Selection Ceremony at dusk.

Mother straightened and stepped back, her appraising gaze taking me in from head to foot.

"You girls are so beautiful." Her eyes crinkled in a tired smile as she looked from me to Lana, who was perched on the edge of Mother's bed. "I'm so relieved this is your last Selection. Even with our clan's pre-arranged Obligate—"

Mother's words cut off as she pressed her fingers to her lips and a rattling cough wracked her body. I guided her to the chair in the corner.

"We should let you rest before the ceremony," Lana said. She stood and moved to the foot of the bed, feeling her way with a light touch of her fingertips over the bed.

"We'll wake you in plenty of time, Mother." I waited until her coughing calmed, and then helped her stand and go to the bed.

Lana went to the doorway and waited while I tucked Mother in and poured water from the pitcher into the heavy ceramic mug on her bedside table.

"She's getting worse again," Lana whispered after I closed the bedroom door.

We moved quietly into to the tiny room that served as kitchen, dining room, and sitting room. Lana pulled her arm from my grasp and went to the chair that was once the color of bergamine skin but had faded to a dusty orange-beige. She could move around our small house without worry of stumbling or running into anything, as we'd had it arranged exactly the same way for years so she could navigate it without help.

"She's just tired," I said. "Selection preparations." Mother had spent the past three days baking rolls to contribute to the Fete and Feast Day.

I stifled a sigh, put on an apron, and turned to the dishes in the sink. In spite of my words, I suspected Lana was right, that Mother was on the verge of another flare-up. With every exacerbation, she became a bit weaker.

A rap on the small window over the sink pulled me from my worries. My hands froze in the suds at the sight of Court's drawn face peering at me.

"I need to talk to you, Maya," he said.

His stance was somber, his hands clasped in front of him. His forehead lined in a contrite expression. He was dressed in his Selection whites and ceremonial cord. The garb accentuated his tan face and the pure whites of his eyes.

"Please?" he said.

I wasn't sure I'd ever heard Court say that word.

I nodded once and dried my hands on the front of my apron.

"Don't you dare take him back," Lana said heatedly.

Her weaving was jumbled in her lap. She turned her head, following the sound of my movement as I took off my apron and left it on a hook by the door.

"I can handle him," I said.

Lana had never approved of my relationship with Court. I'd always told myself it was because she was overly protective, but that had probably just been my way of rationalizing her misgivings. And, I realized, it was also my way of ignoring what I didn't want to see.

I lifted my chin, drew a deep breath, and opened the door.

Court offered a tentative smile when he came around the corner of the house.

Why hadn't he gone to the door and knocked like a normal person instead of creeping around looking for me in the windows? Coward.

I crossed my arms and regarded him in stony silence.

His gaze roamed my body. His smile widened and heat grew in his eyes. "You look . . . you're beautiful, Maya."

Yes, I know. My mother already told me.

When I didn't respond to his compliment, his smile

faltered a bit. He ran one hand up and down the other arm as if to ward off a chill, though it was still muggy and hot. I rather enjoyed seeing him squirm a bit.

He cleared his throat and looked off to the side. "Farrah was . . . she isn't . . . she doesn't mean to me what you do," he said haltingly.

"You had *sex* with her, Court. Often, by the familiarity between the two of you. And with the obvious expectation that you'd be doing it many more times in the future." My heart raced with anger and hurt.

"No, no, you're not seeing it right. I had—I did that with her because I don't care for her the way I care for you. With you I wanted to wait. Just like you always said, so it would be special."

My pulse surged even more at his admission and the feeble reasoning for his betrayal. "In the meantime you were simply using her to satisfy your needs?" I asked.

He brightened and started to nod. Then his eyes widened, and he drew back a little as he took in my horrified reaction. "I don't . . . um . . ."

"So you would have stopped after we were married? Because then you wouldn't need her anymore?" I softened my voice and gave him a completely fabricated look of hope. "You'd be completely faithful to me and never touch another woman again? You'd be with me and only me until the end of your days?"

His mouth pulled down in a sour look before he could

manage to stretch it into a too-wide smile. "Uh, yes, of course."

Lifting a hand, he stepped toward me. When I didn't back away, he moved closer and brushed my cheek with the backs of his fingers.

For a moment I felt myself weaken, felt the pull of Court's beautiful face cloud my mind. A spark of desire lit up deep inside me.

"I'm saving you because you're special. You're the best of all of them, Maya." His voice actually trembled a little.

Any desire I'd felt fled from my body. *Of* all *of them? Exactly how many were there?* I wanted to scream.

Instead, I leaned toward him and looked up from under my lowered lashes. "If you really mean that, meet me here tonight after the Selection. Late, after our parents have gone to sleep," I purred.

He grinned broadly. "I will. I would love that."

He stooped for a kiss, and it was all I could do to keep my fists firmly clamped under my elbows. I sidestepped and gave him a playfully admonishing look. "Not until tonight."

I turned to the door and, after one last coquettish glance at Court over my shoulder, went inside.

Lana wore a sly grin. "Whatever you have planned, he deserves it ten times over." She tipped her head innocently toward her basket of cord dyes.

I allowed myself a chuckle and knelt for the cobalt. Later, I'd offer Court a special glass of wine.

My heart still ached, but a new energy surged through

me. I felt as if I'd started to expand beyond my old self, as if the too-small cocoon that had encased me for as long as I could remember had suddenly become noticeably tight, and I'd begun the process of emerging, raw and tender, into something new.

The ceremony pavilion was nestled on a plateau tucked against a range of foothills at the edge of town not far from our house. Rand's family owned a tiny rattleclap car, and Rand had given up his seat to my mother so she wouldn't have to walk the mile or so uphill to the pavilion.

Rand, Lana, and I walked slowly, trying not to kick up dust on the road, and the deliberate pace gave the long line of citizens and white-clad Obligate Elects a somber, processional feel.

Lana and I strode with our elbows linked, and drew many glances. People's eyes often seemed to want to linger on us when we were together, especially when we were dressed alike. Seeing a matched pair seemed to strike people as interesting or odd, I supposed. And for the ceremony we were a perfectly matched pair, dressed alike and made up with the same hairstyle.

In moments like these, I almost felt as if my twin and I were of one spirit, moving through the world in separate bodies but synchronized with each other on some ethereal plane.

Rand walked on my other side, moving nearer to me when

we spotted Court and his family join the procession. Court twisted, and out of the corners of my eyes, I saw him spot me and felt his gaze linger. I turned toward Lana and mumbled something inconsequential to her, pretending I didn't see Court's searching look.

With Rand close enough that the back of his wrist occasionally brushed mine, I couldn't help comparing him to Court again. The past year and a half it could have been me and Rand getting to know each other, talking and laughing.

But I'd had eyes only for Court.

I looked up at Rand, waited until he turned to me, and then held his gaze. "Thank you for giving my mother your ride to the pavilion, for walking with us, and for offering to escort me tonight."

Thank you for always being there . . . even while I was a girlish idiot.

The look on his face was like the sun bursting out after a day of rain. "Of course." He glanced at my sister. "I'd be glad to escort both of you, that is if Lana isn't already taken."

I elbowed my sister. "She always refuses escort."

Lana turned a soft smile toward Rand. "I just didn't want to get attached before my final Selection Ceremony. It always seemed bad luck . . ." she trailed off with a guilty grimace, realizing what she'd said.

An awkward silence grew between the three of us.

I heaved a deep sigh. "Lana, you've always been the smarter of the two of us. From now on, you are in charge of all of my important decisions." There was no bitterness in my voice, but a pinprick of pain pierced my heart and I couldn't help a glance at Court.

Lana's tinkling laugh broke the tension. "I'm just cautious. You're far more courageous than I am."

I tipped my head toward hers until our temples touched, and squeezed her arm. I couldn't imagine how anyone could survive without a twin.

As the slope of the road steepened, the purples and blues of the evening sky colored the hills. The alabaster ceremony pavilion—a circular structure with tiered seating surrounded by tall columns—stood out starkly against the darker backdrop of the foothills.

A hush seemed to descend over the thick line of people moving up the road.

My thoughts turned to Belinda, the Obligate who would be offered to the Selection from our clan. She'd been born during the same half-year as me and Lana, and though I didn't know her well I could picture her heart-shaped face, pale blonde curls, and delicate hands.

This would have been Belinda's last Selection ceremony before she was free to marry and build a life of her own. Instead, she would be entering the competition in the overlords' city of Calisto. If she survived the competition, she would be rewarded with a slave position on some other world—not much of a reward, but certainly better than death during one of the competition's challenges. If she emerged the overall victor, she would join Lord Toric's harem and live out the rest of her life in luxury and service to the Lord. But no matter what the outcome, she would never return home.

I sent up a prayer to the overlords and the stars above, asking that Belinda be filled with strength and courage. And another prayer for her family, for making such a profound sacrifice.

There were many bowed heads around me, and I guessed that others were silently reciting similar prayers.

As if those battling far overhead had sensed our prayers, a silent explosion lit high in the sky. I stiffened as I watched fiery debris streak through the atmosphere.

My heart jolted at the sight of the flames streaking toward land, even though I knew any debris that didn't burn up would hit the protective shield and bounce away or slide to the ground outside the protected zones.

The invocation went up around the crowd. "Praise the overlords, praise Lord Toric."

I joined in, repeating the phrase three times.

If not for the protection of the overlords, we on Earthenfell would have perished many hundreds of years ago as alien races fought to claim our planet. The battles in the skies have raged for centuries, but the overlords have kept us safe, fighting our enemies so we could live in peace.

We had no deep love for the overlords and did not worship them, but we knew that without them we'd all be dead. And so we always praised them.

I shivered, imagining how vast and terrifying it must be up there beyond the shield. I sent up another prayer, one of protection for the overlord fighters who tirelessly fended off our enemies.

When we passed under the arch to enter the pavilion, I scanned the section our clan was assigned until I spotted my mother sitting in the third row.

"I see Mother," I said to Lana. I looked up at Rand. "Thank you again for allowing her to ride with your family. I'm not sure she could have come otherwise."

"Of course, Maya." He gave a little bow of his head, touched my elbow, and then angled off toward his own clan's section.

I guided Lana through the aisles, past other clan groupings. There was a charged energy in the air despite the hush, and my stomach tightened with nervous anticipation.

When we passed a clan section where a man stood with a bucket in his arms, from which his clan's Obligate would be drawn by lottery, I shivered. I couldn't imagine what that clan's Obligate Elects must be feeling, knowing that after the feast, one of them would have to leave their home forever and go to Calisto with no preparation or training to compete.

Mother gave us a tired smile when we reached the section with the Clan Terra banner. I let Lana sit in between us, and I turned to wave at a couple of distant cousins farther up in the Clan Terra seating who were also wearing Obligate Elect white.

At one time, everyone in a clan was related somehow. But

through the centuries, the bloodlines crossed and mixed so much it became too difficult to draw lines between them based on blood relation. The clans later became symbolic groupings rather than family groupings, though most people had at least a few relatives in the same clan.

I noticed the front-most row of our section was conspicuously empty.

"Have you seen Obligate Belinda yet?" I asked Mother in a hushed tone.

She shook her head. "Neither her nor her family," she rasped, and then coughed a few times.

I frowned. By Clan Terra tradition, our Obligate usually arrived early to the pavilion. Before the ceremony began, all of Clan Terra's Obligate Elects would line up and file past to offer the Obligate a prayer of thanks and strength. We did that while the lottery clans chose their Obligates by drawing.

It wouldn't feel right to skip the traditional prayer for our Obligate.

My unease mounted as the pavilion continued to fill. All of the Obligate Elects—young men and women between the ages of eighteen and twenty—stood out from the rest in their white ceremonial garb. There were sixteen clans total, and sixteen Obligates would be offered.

But where was ours?

The sky had deepened to the violet blue of dusk, and the crowd was settling as the last few attendees found places with their clans.

Down on the pavilion's stage the light bearers had lined up, eight on each side, one for each of the sixteen Obligates who would go to Calisto for our half-year's Selection.

I watched as Mr. Arsen, the Clan Terra officiant for the Selection seated in our clan's first row, twisted and scanned our section. His salt-and-pepper eyebrows were drawn together, forming a deep vertical worry crease in the center of his forehead.

I glanced at Mother. She was watching Mr. Arsen, too.

An anguished cry pulled my attention toward the section to our left. A woman about my mother's age was clutching at a young man who was dressed in Obligate Elect white. The young man stood stiff and still, a stricken look frozen on his face. Nearby, an officiant with a lottery bucket held a slip of paper.

I swallowed hard as I watched the young man look down at the woman who was silently sobbing against his chest.

"This is my duty, Mother," he said. His voice was strong and clear, but his expression was dazed and his eyes glassy and wide.

Lana tilted her head and then turned to me. "Who was the young man drawn for that clan?"

I squinted, trying to place him. He looked familiar. We'd been in school together; he was a year behind me if I remembered correctly. I didn't think I'd crossed paths with him since Lana and I had graduated. "He's younger than us. Orion, I think is his name?"

She nodded solemnly. "Yes. I remember the name. I think he may have ended up in machinery."

Orion's sleeves were tight around his biceps as he raised his hands to his mother's shaking back and bent to touch his cheek to the top of her head. His shoulders looked well-muscled, too. If he had indeed been working on one of the machinery lines for the past year, his job had given him a very fit physique. That would help him when he went to Calisto to compete to become one of Lord Toric's personal servants.

My heart ached for him and for his mother, who was trying to compose herself but still trembled as she wiped her eyes.

There were similar scenes in the other sections where Obligates were being drawn by lottery.

I inhaled a slow breath and trained my attention on the stage, feeling unnerved. I wasn't sure why I felt shaken by the scene. It was my fourth Selection ceremony as an Obligate Elect, and I'd attended the Selection since the age of ten like all of the other Earthenfell children. I knew exactly what to expect. Perhaps it was the gouge in my heart left by Court's betrayal that made everything else feel more raw.

Movement in one of the aisles caught my eye. A boy of about fourteen years old was taking the steps two at a time. He stopped, his chest heaving and sweat beading on his forehead, in front of Mr. Arsen. The boy leaned down to say something in Mr. Arsen's ear.

Despite the evening heat, a chill swept through my body. Everything seemed to slow as I watched Mr. Arsen stand and face us. His face was pale, his jaw slack. He clamped his mouth closed, swallowed, and then held one hand up high.

"Clan Terra," he said, his voice carrying up the tiers. "Our Obligate—" He faltered and his eyes bugged wide. He gave a slight shake of his head. "Obligate Belinda has—has died. Of a snake bite. Only an hour ago."

My hand flew to my mouth as a chorus of gasps and cries rose around me. I turned to my mother and sister, and their faces reflected my own horror.

Being close to the front, I could see Mr. Arsen's lips tremble as he raised his other arm and then flapped both hands, encouraging us to quiet down.

He turned and beckoned to the boy, who stood off to the side, watching. Cries and questions burst out in our section, creating an anxious cacophony.

Ignoring my mother's distressed voice and Lana's clutching fingers on my arm, and remained transfixed. Mr. Arsen said something to the boy and he nodded. With his head down, he sidestepped past Mr. Arsen. He went to the section to our left and tapped the shoulder of Orion's clan officiant.

The officiant handed his clan's lottery bucket to the boy, and the boy jogged back to Mr. Arsen.

"We have no choice," Mr. Arsen said, taking the bucket from the boy. "We must draw our Obligate by lottery."

3

Maya

MY THROAT WENT dry and my heart seemed to falter for a few beats. Then everything sped up, my pulse raced, and the shocked voices all around me thundered in my ears.

For a second or two, I tried to guess how many Obligate Elects there were in our clan, tried to calculate my and Lana's odds of getting selected. There were certainly at least a couple dozen of us. But fewer than forty, maybe? My brain refused to complete the estimate.

Lana was clinging to my arm with both hands. Mother was looking around like a lost child, wide-eyed and open-mouthed.

My eyes kept slipping over to Orion, the Obligate whose name had been drawn only moments ago from the bucket that Mr. Arsen held.

Orion had moved to the bottom row of the section for his clan—Clan Cairns. He sat with his chin up, his spine straight, and a hand resting on each thigh. Some members of his clan gathered around him to offer a few words and then drifted back to their seats. Orion nodded at each one. I couldn't quite see his full profile from where I sat, but there was an admirable dignity to his posture.

I flicked a glance back down at Mr. Arsen, who'd enlisted a few Clan Terra members to help him quickly scribble names on the backs of the pieces of paper that Clan Cairns had used for their lottery.

"How could Obligate Belinda have been bitten by a snake on Selection day of all days?" The sound of Lana's shocked voice made me turn to her.

I shook my head slowly. "I can't imagine," I said, barely managing enough air to push the words out.

"What about the next Clan Terra Obligate in line? Teresa? Can't she go in Belinda's place?" Lana asked.

"No. Teresa won't be of age until the next Selection." Teresa was slated to go to Calisto as Clan Terra's Obligate in her first Selection next spring. She was still only seventeen and thus still ineligible for that evening's the Selection.

I glanced again at my twin. If we'd allowed the overlords to classify Lana as a disabled citizen, she would have been taken from our home and placed in special housing. But she also would have been safely ineligible for the Selection. I'd always believed that we'd made the right choice, that she was better off at home with us, and truth be told, I couldn't imagine sending her away. I couldn't imagine life without her.

But as I watched Mr. Arsen and the others drop pieces of paper into the lottery bucket, my heart contracted, tightening into a tiny hard pebble of fear in my chest. Had we made the right choice with Lana . . . ?

Mr. Arsen held the lip of the bucket in one hand and shook it back and forth a little. Clan Terra had gone so silent I could hear the quiet rustling of the pieces of paper.

He held the bucket up at shoulder height and nodded at the boy who had delivered the news of Belinda's death. The boy reached up and his hand disappeared into the bucket. He pulled it out and passed a piece of paper to Mr. Arsen.

Mr. Arsen set the bucket down and then gripped the piece of paper in both hands as if it weighed as much as a brick. His lips parted and his chest rose and fell once before he looked up.

"Maya Calderon." He held up the piece of paper.

A roar rose in my ears, the internal sound of my own disbelief and horror. But even through the roar, a thread of relief laced through my heart. At least it was not Lana.

"Maya, no!" Lana's panic was a visceral shot to my heart, but her voice unfroze my limbs.

Mother was gasping, her mouth opening and closing as if she were drowning. She half-rose to her feet and started to cry out, but her words dissolved into a fit of violent coughing and she sank back down.

"Stay right here with Mother," I said softly right next to Lana's ear as calmly as I could manage. I peeled her fingers from my arm and stood, stepping out of the range of her reaching hands.

On clumsy-weak legs, I side-stepped to the aisle and went down to Mr. Arsen. He watched me with huge eyes.

I stiffly moved to stand beside him and face my clan. The weight of their shocked stares seemed to hit me right in the middle of my chest, and I couldn't draw enough breath.

"Maya Calderon," he called out loud enough for the whole section to hear, his voice cracking. He cleared his throat. "Maya Calderon has been selected as Clan Terra's Obligate."

Low words passed through the crowd, like a chill breeze rattling dry limbs, spreading from the lower rows to the upper rows.

I could hear the sounds of my mother and twin weeping and tried to keep my gaze averted, but I couldn't help looking at them. They clung to each other, their faces twisted in unchecked misery.

"Maya," Lana sobbed, as if she could feel my eyes on her.

The anguish in her voice ripped through me, snatching away my resolve with sharp claws. Hands reached out to steady me before I even realized I'd nearly fallen. I tried to hold myself up, but my knees refused to support me.

The hands on my arms and around my waist turned me and lowered me to the center of the front bench of Clan Terra's section, sitting me in the place where Obligate Belinda was supposed to be.

Ahead, the light bearers walked in synchronized steps from each side of the stage to the row of candelabra at the back, marking the beginning of the Selection ceremony. One light bearer for each of the sixteen candles.

One of those candles was for me.

The light bearers filed off the stage, and the Selection Controller, a round woman with gray-streaked hair pulled up in a tight bun at the crown of her head, walked up the five steps from the pit in front of the stage. From there I could just make out the dot of the implant at the back of her neck. Like the man who took our bergamine collections every workday, she was an Earthen but also a direct underling of the overlords. She stood under the rusted iron ceremonial arch, a relic from before the overlords returned to protect Earthenfell, and turned to face the crowd.

Even when the Controller began to speak, the misery of Mother's and Lana's soft sobs still filled my ears, blotting out all other sounds.

Though my ears refused to listen, I knew, more or less, the script the Controller recited. The story of a perilous time before the overlords, back when Earthenfell was called Earth. The near extinction of humans at the hands of violent alien races vying for control of our planet. The arrival of the Calistan overlords, their promise of protection, the raising of the shield, and the battles in the sky.

And the price they demanded: sixteen human Obligates

twice a year.

Suddenly the Controller's words cut through the buzzing in my ears and the sounds of mother's and Lana's grief.

"And so we make this offering twice a year," the Controller said. "We offer sixteen of our own who are in their prime at the command of the overlords and for the pleasure of Lord Toric."

A violent tremor passed through me.

For the pleasure of Lord Toric.

One of the female Obligates would serve the alien lord's pleasure. I realized with a jolt that I did not know for sure what that meant. We would be competing for a position in Lord Toric's harem, of course, but I did not know *exactly* what it meant to serve him.

There were rumors of Lord Toric's enormous sexual appetites. But what kinds of acts did he expect—*demand*—from his harem?

The uncertainty of what lay ahead and the horrible ripping in my heart at the prospect of leaving my home, my family, seemed to be trying to turn me inside out.

My stomach constricted but my lungs felt too wide. My breath hitched as if the muscles around my chest and throat had gone out of sync. I gasped as my pulse raced at a sickening pace.

I looked around wildly for help.

Was I dying like Belinda? Was it a cursed position that would continue to claim Clan Terra Obligates one by one?

Someone laid a hand on my arm and asked me a question,

but I couldn't focus. My breath was hitching so violently I couldn't have responded anyway.

I couldn't breathe. I had to get out.

Flinging concerned hands away, I rose and pitched forward, aiming to run. I made it only a few steps before my feet tangled.

"Easy." A low, soothing voice and a strong arm around my waist cut through my panic.

I looked up into Orion's eyes. He was bent over me with a mix of concern and sympathy on his face. Even in my anguish, I thought how remarkable it was that he could be so kind when he'd learned of his own fate only moments before I'd learned of mine.

With a light touch of one hand on the small of my back and his other hand under my elbow, he guided me back to my clan.

"Slow breaths in through your nose," he whispered.

I did as he instructed. It was a tiny relief just to have something to focus on.

"Your mother and sister need you to be strong. You can do this, Maya." His hand slipped from my elbow, down the underside of my forearm, and squeezed my fingers with gentle pressure before he stepped back and returned to his own clan.

I tried to thank him, but all that came out was a wheezy whisper. The Controller was still speaking. I tried to focus on her words, to pull myself together.

Orion was right. Falling apart would not help Mother and

Lana. I took a steady breath and tried to relax my clenched hands in my lap. My family would need every bit as much strength as I would to survive after I was gone.

My heart lurched with a sickening thump. Lana. Who would fulfill her quota each day?

Just as the new, deep worry began to fill me, someone was pushing at the back of my shoulder.

"You must go down there now." Mr. Arsen was urging me to rise.

I started to stand so I could go join the other Obligates who were descending through the aisles to gather in the pit in front of the stage, but my knees gave out.

"Maya." A hand appeared. I knew from the voice that it was Orion.

I grasped his hand and let him haul me to my feet. I stood there a moment, making sure my legs would hold me. Then I nodded to Orion.

"Thank you." I pulled my shoulders back and lifted my chin, and he let go.

He held out one palm, indicating that I should go ahead of him in the aisle that led to steps down the side of the pavilion seating.

My first few breaths were shaky and constricted as I left my clan and my family behind. But as I walked, I concentrated every bit of strength on steeling myself. I wanted Mother and Lana to see how steadily I moved, how calm I was.

The steps down to the stage seemed to stretch out forever,

but I focused on one at a time. It helped to know that Orion was right behind me. Two other Obligates walked down the steps ahead of me, and I wondered if they'd spent the past couple of years preparing for such a moment, or if they were like me and Orion.

"Maya?" Someone in the seats exclaimed. It was a familiar voice.

I slowed and turned my head, and my eyes met Rand's. His mouth fell open and his head tipped to the side just a fraction, as if he were struggling to understand what he saw.

I averted my eyes, staring down at the next step. I had to focus my entire effort on keeping my composure.

Rand. Maybe he could help Lana. It was a huge request, but he was the type of man who just might do it. My heart lifted just a hair.

As the stage loomed ahead, I darted a look at the other Obligates converging at the bottom of the stairs the Selection Controller had climbed to begin the ceremony. My mind blanked. What was I supposed to do? I'd watched the ceremony many times before, of course, but for some reason my mind could not translate what I'd witnessed as an onlooker into what I should do as a participant.

I stopped behind the Obligate in front of me, a curvy young woman several inches shorter than me with waves of hair that hung halfway down her back. Auburn hair, I could see we were close enough to the candles.

I stared up at the stout Controller who surveyed us with

grave eyes, her hands clasped under her large breasts.

"Obligates, take your places of honor." She stepped a few paces to one side and swept one arm out, inviting us up.

I remembered. The Clan Terra Obligate always stood behind the third candle from the right. I moved into the right hand line that was forming, positioning myself so that I'd end up in the correct spot when we filed on stage in two lines that would split with one going to either side.

On stage, I took my place behind the third candle. With the brightness of the flame in my eyes, I could barely make out the people in the audience. They were mostly just rows of faceless forms, and for that I was grateful.

Court came to my mind, the thought of him quite unwelcome but the habit of him still too firmly in my heart. What was he thinking, seeing me on stage? That with me gone he'd be truly free now? He wouldn't even have to answer any awkward questions about why he and I weren't together anymore, why we weren't going to marry. I was an Obligate, gone and forever out of reach. How convenient for him.

The Controller had reclaimed her position in the front center of the stage.

"People of Earthenfell, look upon these Obligates, these sons and daughters who are in their prime, and know their sacrifice. With every breath, keep them in your hearts and know it is because of their sacrifice that we continue to enjoy the protection of the overlords."

And then the entire pavilion took up the incantation,

repeating it three times. "Praise the overlords, praise Lord Toric."

Everyone repeated it except the sixteen of us lined up on stage. By tradition, for such a moment we were exempt from praising the overlords.

The ceremony ended, and I exited the stage along with the other Obligates. It was full dark, and I looked around, dazed and fog-headed, unsure of what to do next.

People touched my shoulder, even my cheek as they passed, offering murmured prayers. I ignored them, standing on my tiptoes and searching in vain for my mother and sister. I felt so lost, a leaf swept away by the current.

My eyes stung with the threat of tears. I blinked them back and clamped my teeth down hard on my lips. I wasn't going to cry. Not in front of all these people.

But I didn't have the strength to hold in my tears and search for my family. Feeling drained and hollow, I sank down on the step where I stood, crossed my arms over my knees, and rested my head on my arms.

People touched my back, my head, moving around me. I didn't care.

Then I felt someone close, heard a rustle of clothing. I looked up. Rand was kneeling in front of me.

He slipped an arm around my back and pulled me up. I didn't have the energy to ask him where he was taking me. People moved out of the way as he guided me out of the pavilion.

He moved his hand from my back to my shoulder and pulled me into the crook of his arm. When I saw his family's car and my mother and sister waiting beside it, I fell forward into a run.

Remembering what Orion had advised—to help them be strong—I swallowed back a sob as I went to them and engulfed them in my arms.

Rand, his parents, and his younger sister stood several feet away, giving us some privacy.

It was too dark to see the details of Lana's face, but by her thick, heavy breaths she probably hadn't stopped crying since Mr. Arsen had called my name. Mother's breaths were congested and raspy.

I placed a hand on my mother's cheek. "We need to get you home. You need rest," I said, as if it were any other evening.

I squeezed into the back seat next to them, with Lana in the middle. Rand's father came to the driver's side and silently slid in behind the wheel. Rand's mother reached back from the front passenger seat and clasped my hand for a long moment. She mumbled something tearful that I didn't quite catch.

I glimpsed moonlight highlighting the contours of Rand's face as we rolled away from the pavilion. He walked next to his younger sister, and they both watched somberly as we passed.

The ride home seemed to pass in a blink, and I felt strangely numb to time.

When Rand's father stopped the car in front of our small house and got out to open the door for us, the rowdy laughs and other sounds of merry-making clanged in my ears. The sounds were so at odds with my new reality, they made me wince as if each one were a paper cut on my skin.

I thought of past Selections, when I'd joined in with the celebration while there were Obligates who were feeling anguish and dread too deep to put into words. I'd always been one of the revelers dancing and drinking late into the night. Jubilant . . . smiling . . . carefree. It seemed so wrong now.

Entering our dark house, I felt like a stranger. I stood just inside the doorway, my elbow linked with Lana's, as Mother rummaged around for candles and matches. It was tradition to only use candles for illumination the night of the Selection.

Lana rested her head on my shoulder as Mother lit three candles in the small living room and then turned to us. She looked back and forth between me and Lana, and then her face crumpled like a wadded paper bag.

She rushed to us, and we embraced in a tight circle of tears and silent grief.

It was Mother who pulled back first. She swiped her fingers under her eyes, though more tears quickly replaced the ones she wiped away.

"I can't imagine living a day without you, my daughter." She drew a deep, quivering breath. "But I know that what's done is done, and there's no going back."

Lana had remained pinned to my side, but she separated herself just a little. "I don't know what divine forces decided that I deserved you, my twin, my other half." She reached out and touched my cheek as naturally as if she could see my face. "But I'm so—so . . . *grateful* for the years we've had together." Her halting words stopped as she choked on a sob and fresh tears spilled down her cheeks.

I pulled her to me and held her so tightly I could hardly tell where I stopped and she began. The thought of waking up each day without her was simply too much to bear, so I pushed it firmly away.

Mother went to the kitchen and rummaged in a cupboard as Lana's crying subsided. I led my sister to the narrow sofa and sat down next to her.

"I've been saving this wine for tonight." Mother lifted a dark bottle. In her other hand she held three chipped goblets upside down with the stems between her fingers. "I can think of no reason why we shouldn't drink it."

By the label, it looked to be a mid-range vintage. She must have saved for years to be able to buy it.

A tremulous smile passed over her face as she set the bottle and goblets on the side table. "Your father and I drank this label for our wedding day feast." She went back to the kitchen and returned brandishing a bottle opener.

I barely remembered my father. In my mind he was more an impression of the senses than a real person—the rough stubble that scratched my nose when he kissed me soundly on my cheek, the rich aroma of pipe smoke that clung to his clothes, the twinkle in his green eyes when he smiled, the rolling peal of his hearty laugh. He died when Lana and I were very young.

"I wish he were still here," I whispered. "So that I would know he was taking care of you after I'm gone."

The last three words I'd spoken seemed to ring out in the room, even though I'd said them quietly. *After I'm gone.* It sounded so final. It felt like a pronouncement of death.

Mother splashed some wine into a goblet and quickly tipped it back, emptying it. Then she filled it again, as well as the other two. I put one into Lana's hands.

Mother looked down into her goblet for a moment. "I wish he were still here, too." Loss weighed so heavily on her face, and I could hardly bear it.

"A toast," I said, my voice wavering. I held up my goblet. "May we all find what peace we can, collect as many moments of happiness as possible, and know gratitude in every breath."

We tapped the rims of our goblets against each other. When the wine spread over my tongue, the rich citrus, bitter, and sweet notes battled each other for dominance. It was the most delicious thing I'd ever tasted. I drank, savoring each swallow, until it was gone.

"This is wonderful," Lana murmured.

I expected mother to cork the bottle, but instead she filled our glasses again. Halfway into my second glass, a tingling warmth seeped into my limbs and a pleasant numbness began to crowd into my head.

Just as I had nearly polished off another cupful, there was a rap at the door. I rose to answer it, and pitched a little before steadying myself.

I opened the door to Rand, his hands clasped in front of him and his silhouette framed by the dark night.

"I—I wasn't sure if I should . . ." He trailed off and swallowed.

I smiled, genuinely happy to see him, and grabbed his wrist and pulled him inside. "Oh nonsense," I said. "I'm very glad you came."

A tentative smile began to widen his lips, but when he caught sight of my mother and sister, his expression sobered. He ducked his head. "Mrs. Calderon, Lana, I know you've had a terrible shock tonight. I can't imagine how you must be feeling right now."

Lana managed a little smile, and her cheeks pinked. "We're certainly better than we were before Mother opened that bottle of wine."

"Please, have some with us." Mother hurried to the kitchen and came back with another goblet, splashed a bit of wine in it, and handed it to Rand.

He took it with a conflicted look on his face and glanced at me.

"It's amazing, please enjoy it," I said, and nodded encouragingly at the goblet he held.

I drained the last of my own wine and turned to Mother and Lana. "Would you mind very much if I went out for a while? I just want to walk around a bit. And seeing as how Rand was kind enough to offer to escort me . . ."

Mother was already flapping her hands at us, making shooing motions. "Yes, of course, and you should try to enjoy yourselves for a bit."

A look of eager happiness sparked in Rand's eyes, and he tipped his goblet up, quickly consuming its contents in a few swallows. "Thank you so much for the wine, it was indeed delicious."

I set his empty goblet next to mine and led him to the door.

I was extremely grateful he'd still come for me. I had two important things that I hoped he could help me with. One was the issue of Lana and her quotas in the orchards.

And the other, well . . . in the course of a day I'd lost so much. My innocence had slipped away like a thin veil stolen by the wind in a storm. It seemed fitting to take one more step to complete the transformation before I had to leave Earthenfell forever. I'd made up my mind that by daybreak, I would no longer be a virgin.

4
Maya

WHEN I SHUT the front door, darkness enveloped me and Rand like a lightweight cloak. I felt for his hand, and his fingers closed firmly around mine.

"I hope I didn't overstep," he said, a nervous tremor in his voice. He squeezed my hand a couple of times. "But whether you still wanted me to escort you or not, there was no way I could let the night pass without at least checking on you. And I couldn't—well, I couldn't let you go without seeing you again."

"No, I'm truly glad you came." I hoped that the warmth I felt for him was evident in my voice.

We walked slowly, passing homes lit from within only by the rosy-yellow flickers of candlelight. The sound of laughter drifted to us from a porch a few houses away. A door slammed nearby, and from the direction of mid-town, a raucous burst of laughter went up. The late summer night was still and warm enough that dampness formed between my palm and Rand's.

"Where would you like to go?" he asked. "I'm happy to take you to the heart of the revelry in mid-town, but I assumed that might be a bit . . . too much."

The wine was making my head swim and my muscles pleasantly tingly. "I think I would like a bit of bread. Perhaps more wine. Maybe one of the pubs that's on the edge of mid-town?"

"Your wish is my command," Rand said with a smile in his voice.

He shifted closer to me and, after a few moments, let go of my hand and slipped his arm around my waist in a comforting gesture.

As we left the residential neighborhoods and drew closer to mid-town, the sounds of celebration grew louder. But unlike before when the noises felt like a jarring assault on my ears, they lifted my spirits. Perhaps it was the wine, or Rand's company. Or perhaps the initial shock of my fate had worn off and acceptance was taking its place. Maybe it was a combination of all of these things. Regardless, I was glad for the shift because I didn't want to spend my last night on Earthenfell in complete despair, and I was glad that Rand didn't bring up the subject of my departure.

He guided me through the dark streets, and I was content to let him choose our route. We reached a neighborhood that was a mix of residences, pubs, and small specialty shops. The shops were all closed, but the pubs were well lit with dozens of candles and lively with people.

The door of a pub, the Rusty Nail, stood open. My pulse tapping nervously, I slowed a little as we neared it.

"Ready?" Rand asked, looking down at me.

I paused and then nodded, and he moved his arm so I could walk in ahead of him.

Inside, I tried to take in everything with one sweeping look—people drinking, eating, and laughing. A lively game of cards was going at the table in the corner. Every table was full, and people lined the bar. The smell of roasted meat and grilled vegetables permeated the air. My stomach rumbled.

A man standing at a tall, round-topped table near the doorway looked up and nodded at us, and then did a double-take.

"Aye!" he shouted, turning to the barkeep and waving to get his attention. "Aye! We are graced with the presence of an Obligate here!"

The barkeep looked up from the mug he was filling from a tap. He set the mug down, wiped his hands on his apron, and then held up both arms.

"Patrons, patrons!" he called out, and then waited for shushes to pass through the crowd. "Here we are joined by Obligate . . ." He looked to me.

"Maya Calderon," I supplied in the silence that had fallen over the pub.

"Obligate Maya Calderon," the barkeep intoned. "We give

you our thanks, our blessings, and our highest praise."

My breath caught in my throat as every voice in the pub repeated the traditional phrase.

Three men beckoned us over and then moved aside, leaving me and Rand to take their table. I nodded my thanks, and before I was even settled in my chair, plates of food and mugs of brew appeared before us.

A bit dazed from the attention, I picked at the piece of bread balanced on the edge of my plate. The food smelled delicious, but my stomach wasn't ready for a large meal.

And I was distracted, too, with thoughts of my other plans for the night. My stomach tightened in a sense of anticipation that was something between nervousness and eagerness.

Rand seemed rather uninterested in his food as well. He took a few bites and glanced around every so often when a particularly loud guffaw or exclamation rose over the crowd, but otherwise he had eyes only for me.

We talked of inconsequential things—the good flavor of the year's autumn brew, the fine weather we had for the Fete— and he entertained me with some stories of when he first started as a fruit picker in the orchards and couldn't climb a tree to save his life.

After a while he crossed his arms on the table and leaned forward, his eyes intent on mine. "Would you like to get out of here?"

I nodded and warmth rose to my cheeks.

He stood and held out his hand in an almost formal

gesture. I placed my hand in his, stood, and fought back the urge to giggle nervously.

Rand smiled down at me and then glanced toward the doorway. His expression abruptly soured, and his eyes pinched to slits. I followed his gaze.

Court stood just inside the pub. I saw the flash of Farrah's red-orange hair just past his shoulder, and then she stepped beside him and into my full view. My eyes dropped to their clasped hands.

Court yanked his hand from Farrah's. His lips hung open in a small oval as he stared at me.

A mix of ire, hurt, and the desire to be anywhere else twisted my insides. But instead of shrinking, I pulled myself straight and lifted my chin.

Court's eyes widened as I strode straight for him.

"Maya, I'm—I'm . . ." he stammered.

I just looked him straight in the eye for a long moment. Farrah was grasping at his arm and trying to get his attention, but he shook her off.

He swallowed. "Could we talk? Just for a minute?" His eyes darted from me to Rand and back to me again.

I nodded and then turned and went to Rand, raised to my tiptoes, and kissed him on the cheek. "I'll only be a moment, I promise."

Court and I brushed by Farrah. He paid her no more than a distracted glance, despite the furious look on her face and the stiff way she stood with her arms crossed.

I went a few feet away from the door, just beyond the rectangle of soft light that spilled through the doorway.

Spinning on him, I shifted my weight to one hip and planted a hand on the side of my waist. "What do you want?"

He flinched at my abrupt turn. Rubbing the back of his neck with one hand, he flicked a glance at the doorway, then leaned toward me and tried on a contrite look that I didn't quite buy. "Maya, I feel bad, truly awful, about what happened between us. Especially now that you're—"

"You *betrayed* me, Court," I cut him off. "It wasn't something that happened *between* us. It was you—only you— who lied to me and snuck around behind my back with Farrah and who knows how many others."

The tip of his tongue passed over his lips and his mouth pursed for a moment, bringing out his dimple. Oh, that dimple. How many times had it undone me up there in the canopy of the orchards?

"You're right, of course," he said with unconvincing regret. "But considering everything you're facing, I just, well, I couldn't leave things that way. I don't want you to think . . . badly . . . of me." It seemed to pain him to say even that, and he hadn't yet come within ten yards of an actual apology.

"Considering everything you've done, what exactly *should* I think of you?"

"I'm not a bad guy!" he exclaimed, as he held up his arms and an exasperated look replaced any pretense of remorse.

"No, you're a real peach," I said. I was about to leave

Earthenfell forever, and all Court cared about was that I didn't leave thinking ill of him. I narrowed my eyes and lowered my voice. "You know, I meant to spike your brew with cobalt. Maybe Farrah's too. But now I realize that neither of you are worth the tiny effort it would require. You aren't a man. You're a self-indulgent child that no woman will ever be able to depend on."

His face clouded, but then he gave me a tentative raise of his brows. "So, uh, you don't want to meet up later?"

With an exasperated hiss of breath through my clenched teeth, I pushed past him and strode back into the pub, grabbed Rand's hand, and pulled him outside.

My cheeks burned, but not so much due to anger at Court as irritation with myself. How could I have been such an enormous fool over such an insubstantial person? I was glad, actually, that I had seen Court for what he truly was before I had to leave. Had I gone to Calisto thinking that he was some kind of fairy tale prince, I would have pined for him and pitied myself forever for the loss of the life I had dreamed of having with him.

A block or so away from the pub, I slowed to a normal strolling pace. My heart was still racing from the adrenaline of the confrontation. I let out a slow breath and then looked up at Rand and tried to relax my face into a smile, though I knew it was too dark for him to clearly see my expression. "I apologize. I imagine that was a bit awkward for you."

He waved a hand back and forth a couple of times, as if

swatting at a gnat. "Don't give it a second thought. I think it was good that you got the opportunity to say, well, whatever was on your mind."

I gave a short mirthless laugh. "I suppose that's a good way to see it." I paused, debating about whether to make a little confession, and then decided that I had nothing to lose. "I'd actually planned on spiking his brew with cobalt tonight. Before . . . before the Selection, anyway."

He chuckled, and it made me smile in earnest. "Do you still want to do it?" he asked, in all seriousness.

I shook my head. "I don't want to waste any more time on Court."

Rand curled his fingers tighter around mine in response.

We were skirting around mid-town, past a row of dark shops.

"What *would* you like to do?" Rand said.

I swallowed and licked my dry lips. "Actually, I need to speak to you about something. There's the matter of my sister . . ." I trailed off, suddenly too choked up to continue.

I let go of Rand's hand and my shoes softly scuffed to a halt. I closed my eyes and pressed my fingertips over my eyelids, trying to squeeze back the flood of tears that threatened to burst forth.

"Of course I will collect for Lana," he said.

And then my face was against Rand's chest, and his arms encircled my back. He stroked my hair as the dam broke, and I soaked his shirt with tears. In between my shuddering sobs,

I heard the sound of his soothing murmurs.

When my tears subsided, I sniffed sharply and swept my fingers across my wet cheeks. I looked up at him. "I can never thank you enough, Rand."

One of his arms still held me around the waist, and the other had moved from the back of my head to my cheek. I tipped my face up to his, and as if we had the same thought at the same time, we leaned toward each other and our lips met.

Rand's mouth was warm and sensuous against mine, and an unexpected bolt of desire shot through me.

When we parted for a breath, I whispered his name. He responded by kissing me with more force, his fingers moving from my cheek to tangle into my hair. I locked my arms around his neck and rose to my tiptoes.

I could feel my pulse pounding in my lips, behind my eyes, and down my inner thighs. I pressed into him, and he made a low hum of appreciation against my lips.

My mind spun wildly—where could we go, somewhere private?

I pulled back and opened my mouth with the intention of telling him I wanted to go somewhere we could be alone. The moment had arrived. The energy between us was building, and I had the perfect chance to give myself to him as I'd planned. But something stopped me, and instead of carrying through with it, I just stared at him mutely.

I realized that the main reason I'd wanted to lose my virginity was to get back at Court. But what would it really accomplish? It had been *my* choice to wait with Court. Knowing there was no future with him, I needed to do what was right for me. Me alone. Maya without Court.

A fiery burst of light overhead made us both look up. We watched as debris from the battles over Earthenfell streaked through the atmosphere like comets. It was a thrilling and terrifying display.

"Praise the overlords, praise Lord Toric," we said in unison three times.

I took it as confirmation from the universe that I was right to wait, to not give myself to a man in the haphazard way that I'd intended.

I looked into Rand's eyes. "Let's find music. A place to dance until our feet can't hold us up any longer."

His face broke out into a grin, and he grabbed my hand. We found the noisiest part of mid-town, where there was a seven-piece band playing rollicking tunes.

We lost ourselves in the crowded dance floor, and I let the music, the sparkle in Rand's eyes, and the press of bodies sweep away much of my sorrow and fear.

We danced until the early morning hours until the band finally stopped and began to pack up their instruments.

Exhausted and sweaty, we walked hand-in-hand toward Southside Borough. When I realized that Rand had sunk deep in thought, I looked up at him questioningly.

He stopped, moved in front of me, and then grasped both of my hands in his.

"Maya, I—" He cut himself off with a sharp exhale. He swallowed and started again. "It's killing me that this must be the end for us. If you were staying, I would ask you to be my wife."

I started to protest, to beg him to stop speaking because I suddenly couldn't bear to hear the words. I didn't want my mind to jump to that possibility, to envision a life with Rand, when I would be leaving Earthenfell forever in less than a day.

He quickly interrupted me. "I know you do not love me now," he said, clearly misinterpreting my reason for trying to silence him. "But if I'd had the chance, I would have made you so happy and filled your heart with such joy you would have had no choice but to love me."

"Rand, you are a better man than I deserve," I whispered, barely forcing out the words around the lump in my throat.

"Don't say that," he said fiercely. He squeezed my hands so tightly pain flared in my fingers. "You are the most beautiful, kind, and radiant woman on Earthenfell. I've loved you for a decade, and I will love you until the end of my days." His eyes welled in the starlight, but to my relief no tears fell.

I didn't know how to respond. I did care for Rand, but the force of his feelings hit me like a punch to the stomach and it was suddenly too much. On top of everything else, I couldn't bear the weight of his love and the burden of his loss that would come when I left.

I wiggled my fingers to loosen one hand from his grip and reached up to touch his cheek. "It pains me, too, that we will not have the chance." I simply couldn't summon the will to say more.

When I began to step away, his face clouded. I felt bad that he seemed to expect me to say more, but the pull of home was drawing my mind elsewhere. And even though we wouldn't see each other again after I left, it didn't feel right to exaggerate my feelings just to make him feel good. I was as good as gone. The quicker he moved on, the better.

Although we walked hand-in-hand through the dark streets, Rand seemed much more distant than just an arm's length away. A few times, I began to say something to him but then stopped myself, realizing that anything I might say would probably sound inane and inadequate.

The brutal truth was that I couldn't waste any more time or energy on Rand's feelings. Not with what lay ahead for me.

My chest began to tighten as we arrived at my street. How many more times would I come home and open the front door of the house I'd lived in since birth? Maybe once or twice more before I had to leave for Calisto? The thought was so overwhelming, so stark, it nearly took my breath away.

A few steps from my front door, I forced my attention back to Rand. I stopped and tugged on his hand, compelling him to halt and turn toward me. I couldn't return his romantic feelings, but I did owe him my deepest gratitude.

"You have always been so wonderful to me, Rand," I said softly. "I'm sorry that I didn't appreciate it as much as I should have a long time ago. Please don't allow yourself to languish because of my departure. You only have to get through one more Selection, and then you'll be free. You have your whole life ahead of you. You can get engaged, get married, have your own family. And you should."

His thumb swept back and forth over the back of my hand, and he looked down at his shoes. When he looked up at me, there was a gleam in his eye that I wasn't sure how to interpret, but for the briefest of moments, it made me uneasy. Then he blinked and his expression hardened.

He let go of my hand and shoved both of his in his pockets. "I will look after Lana and see that her quotas are taken care of."

Then he put his head down, moved past me, and walked toward the street. I watched him, my mouth dropping open with bewilderment at the abruptness of his departure. When he continued down the street without a backward glance, I snapped my mouth closed and went to the door. Something about the way Rand left felt oddly open-ended, despite what I'd said to him, but I couldn't afford the effort of analysis.

Inside, a candle on a side table had burned almost down to its stubby end. Someone stirred on the sofa—Lana.

I tiptoed inside, but when she sat up I wasn't really sorry that I'd woken her. As always when we were apart for more than a couple of hours, I craved her company. It was almost a physical relief to be in the same room with her again, like stepping into a bit of shade on a hot day.

"What time is it?" she whispered sleepily.

"I'm not sure." As I sat down, she shifted her legs to make room for me. I faced her, pulling my knees up and clasping my arms around them. "It's still dark out. After three but before four, maybe?"

"Did Rand take you to mid-town?" she asked.

She pulled her knees up too, facing me. Bookends. That's what Mother always called us when we sat like that.

"We stopped at a pub for a bite, and then we danced the rest of the night."

"Really," she said, a statement rather than a question. A sly smile formed on her lips and spread to her eyes. "You *just* danced?"

"Just danced."

She giggled. "I could have sworn you intended more than that."

"Shh." I swatted her wrist with the back of my hand and cast a glance toward Mother's closed bedroom door. "We just danced. Nothing more."

"Maybe you *should* have done something more." She snorted a good-natured laugh. "Better Rand than Court, that lying dog."

"Speaking of Court, we ran into him at the pub. With Farrah."

Lana's mouth dropped open and she sucked in some air. "What did you do?"

I recounted the whole conversation, word for word or as close as I could remember, and Lana nodded approvingly when I got to the end.

"Lana," I said, my tone turning serious. "I asked Rand if he would help with your quotas, and he said he would."

"That is more than I would ever expect of someone," she whispered. "Thank you for taking care of me. I don't know how I could ever repay him for something like this."

We were silent for a few seconds, and then Lana shifted. "Did you at least kiss him?"

"Of course, I'm not a total prude."

"And how did he stack up to Court?"

"I give Rand the edge. I didn't expect it, but he has more passion than you'd guess." I couldn't reveal what he'd said about wanting to marry me. It felt too painful, somehow. "I bet he's more than acceptable in bed."

She slapped her hand over her mouth, and we both tried to stifle our childish giggles. It felt so warm and wonderful, laughing with my twin late into the night just as we'd done countless times since we were small.

Then Lana's hands dropped to her lap and her face turned grave. "Maya, I'm scared about what Lord Toric will do to you. The rumors . . ."

I decided not to remind her that Lord Toric's sexual appetites would only be my problem if I survived the competition and won a place in his harem. The fact was, none of us knew the particulars of what he did with his harem. The rumors ranged from unspeakable humiliating acts to bloody rituals to forced orgies . . . every rumor I'd ever heard, every scenario I'd ever imagined, tried to crowd into my mind at once and I sagged against the backrest of the sofa.

The only thing we really knew for certain was that the female Obligates would enter a series of competitions of charm, wit, physical strength and stamina, and of course, sensuality. The women were competing for a place in Lord Toric's harem. The male Obligates were competing to become one of his many personal servants. Some stages of the competition were deadly, so all of us would be competing for our lives.

My stomach knotted as I reached over to grasp Lana's forearm. "Don't worry, I will charm Lord Toric so thoroughly he will want to be *my* slave."

Her lips twitched as if she thought to try to smile, but then her face pinched and her mouth trembled. "I hate them, Maya. I *hate* the overlords for taking you away from me."

A sickening mix of anger, sadness, and fear poured through me in a dark flood. I hated them, too. For stealing my life, my future. For taking me from the only people I cared about. I knew I shouldn't feel that way—we survived on Earthenfell only at the mercy of the overlords' protection. But I couldn't help my anger.

She placed her hand over mine, and for once I was glad she couldn't see my face. I was glad she couldn't see how truly afraid I was.

5

Toric

ON SELECTION DAY I always woke with a raw feeling in the pit of my stomach, as if the soft spot just behind my sternum had been roughly scraped out while I slept. For the people under the shield on Earthenfell, the day of the Selection was a day of ceremony and revelry into the night. For me, it was a reminder of helplessness and terror. A dark anniversary of the day I was taken from my home when I was just a boy. I also thought of it as the anniversary of the death of that boy, for the young man who was returned home four years later was someone different entirely.

The Selection was a fitting way to mark my personal anniversary, in some grim way. Young men and women forced from their homes and families, taken to a strange land and molded into different people. "Molded" was much too kind a word to describe what I endured, but the analogy still held.

I'd awoken early, and the woman in my bed was still asleep. Sytoria lay sprawled beside me, her frame willowy by Earthenfell standards, but petite compared to the average woman of Calisto. She won entry into my harem four years— eight Selection cycles—back. She was clever and manipulative, and worked her way into my bed more nights than any of the others. I saw through her games, but had no interest in calling her out on them. I told myself it was because I didn't care if it was Sytoria or one of the many others who joined me each evening. But that wasn't exactly the truth. From the beginning, Sytoria had sensed what I needed.

I could wake her, of course. I was the Lord of Calisto and she was there to serve me. But I decided to wait until the first morning toll. Not out of any particular generosity or kindness on my part, but to prove to myself that I *could* wait.

It was a charade, though. I could never wait for long.

As if sensing the morning toll would chime soon, Sytoria rolled to her side, facing me. Her hair, a golden shade between dark blonde and light brown, fell in a wave across her cheek, one strand clinging to the lower lip of her full ruby mouth.

The familiar tightness gathered in my chest and the ache of desire welled in my lower abdomen.

Sytoria's eyes opened and her hand snaked under the covers to wrap around me. She squeezed, painfully hard, but still my arousal grew, which brought a look of satisfaction to her face.

She rose from the bed and walked naked to the large wardrobe, opened the doors, and selected two short whips, one for each of her slender hands. Turning to me, she flashed a wicked, knowing smile.

She knew exactly what I wanted, and I hated her for knowing it. I hated that I wanted what she so willingly gave.

As always, my mind slipped far away as my arousal grew. And as always, my body stayed behind to absorb both the pleasure and the punishment.

LATER AFTER SYTORIA had left, I sat cross-legged in front of the altar that occupied one of the small chambers in my quarters. I didn't always pray in the nude, but considering my fate, it felt right. The welts across my back throbbed in time with my pulse, and somehow that felt right, too—another apt marker of the anniversary of my abduction.

The two urns in front of me—one containing soil from Earthenfell and the other containing ashes from the burnt wood of seven varieties of Earthen trees—were among the plainest things in my chambers and probably in the entire palace. But they seemed to call to my very cells, inviting me to reunite with the sacred land of our ancestors.

We would return to Earthenfell, to our ancestral home, but not until our enemies had been destroyed so that we could live there in peace.

It never failed to strike me how ironic it was that our

slaves were allowed to live and work on the sacred soil of our homeland, but we, their overlords, were forbidden to touch the ground. It was our punishment for abandoning Earth so long ago, for leaving our home behind to range far out into the galaxy. And hundreds of years ago, it became our motivation— we battled for the right to let the shield fall and reclaim our sacred homeland for ourselves.

I clasped my hands and bowed my head. After several breaths to allow my mind to silence, I quietly recited prayers to Mother Earth. I asked for forgiveness for our ancestors' abandonment of Earth. Forgiveness for their hubris in thinking that there was a better home somewhere out there, so many generations ago. I asked for strength for our military commanders and our soldiers fighting for our homeland. And I asked for relief from the demons of my past.

"Toric!" a rough voice jarred me from my meditation.

Every muscle in my body strung tight at the sound of my brother's voice and tighter when he barged noisily into my prayer room.

"Did Sytoria manage to quench your desire this morning?" The corner of my brother's mouth lifted ever so slightly in the subtlest of sneers. His eyes grazed my back, and I suddenly wished I'd gotten dressed. He smirked openly. "I see she gave it her best effort."

His loathing toward me was nothing more than a replay of countless similar scenes between us. But it was still gratingly unpleasant.

When I'd disappeared all those years ago, Jeric had been named my father's heir. The palace, the harem, the servants, and the title of Guardian Lord of Calisto and Earth all would have passed to my brother if I hadn't returned home. He hated me for surviving and resented me for returning to Calisto to claim the title, and he never let me forget it.

All Calistans learned in childhood to mask their energy signatures, and it became as natural as breathing. If I could sense Jeric's, I had no doubt I would feel hot, rolling waves of hate-filled envy.

I rose, facing him with my hands on my hips. Despite the anger flaring through me, I regarded him with cool detachment. "What is so important that you'd interrupt my worship?"

Jeric snorted. Nothing in his expression or stance held a shred of apology for the interruption. He didn't put much credence in worship, though he always went through the motions for the sake of appearance.

"Mother is insisting the council move their daily forum up an hour to accommodate the arrival of the Earthen Offered this afternoon." Jeric lifted a shoulder as if the subject bored him. But I knew better. He coveted Earthenfell women. But they were not for him, and it drove him nearly mad with a jealously that blazed up like a solar flare at the time of each Selection.

I brushed past him and went into my bed chamber. "Fine," I said, hoping a brief, ambivalent response would give him the hint to go.

Of course, it didn't. He followed, sat on the edge of my bed, and then flopped back, mussing the silken cover that one of the servants had straightened while I'd been in prayer.

He stared up at the ceiling. "How many screws have you had in this bed since father passed?" he asked in a mild, musing tone. I knew that voice. It wasn't nearly as harmless as it sounded.

"Not the sort of thing I would track," I said.

I went to the small dressing chamber that was just outside my bathing room, where one of my servants had laid out underclothes, loose-fitting pants, and a shirt made of natural-dyed cotton. Another perk of my station: I was the only Calistan allowed—required, in fact—to wear clothing made only of Earthenfell-grown fibers.

"The notches across your back might help with a rough count." Jeric's voice was still mild, but his words were cutting and meant to provoke me. He knew that any lashes on my body were mended and erased each day.

I emerged from my dressing chamber fully clothed, my patience used up. "Tell Mother I'll be on time. Get out—now."

"Ouch, you're so touchy." He sat up and winced with mock pain, curling his shoulder inward as if I'd made a move to strike him. "Sytoria should have worked you over a little longer."

I stood with my fists at my sides and glared while he took his time standing up and slinking to the door.

I turned away and inhaled deeply as violence tried to rush

up through me. The Guardian Lord of Calisto and Earth was supposed to be grounded and noble. My father had embodied those characteristics with ease, it had always seemed to me. But my father hadn't endured what I had—four years of torture at the hands of our enemies.

I forced my thoughts away from my brother and the Offered who would be coming. Perhaps among them would be a woman who could cure me of my dependence on Sytoria. I should have included *that* in my morning prayers.

6

Maya

THE DAY AFTER the Selection was always a highly anticipated day of feasting, but I found that I could not eat. The delicious smells of cooking meats, arrays of colorful fruits and vegetables, and a variety of crusty breads and rolls were enticing, but my stomach had been clenched into a hard knot since I'd awakened on the sofa.

Lana had stayed on the sofa with me all night and comforted me when I burst into tears as soon as I awoke. For some reason, the realization that I'd spent my last night on Earthenfell on the sofa instead of in the bedroom Lana and I had shared since birth made me desperately sad. I couldn't explain it to her, but she seemed to understand all the same.

I'd composed myself by the time Mother was up. She kissed my forehead and patted my cheek, and if not for the haunted look in her eyes, it might have been any other Saturday. I drank a bit of the coffee she made, trying to avoid the awful realization that I'd never experience another Saturday morning at home, but of course unable to think of anything else.

When a knock came at the door, my heart clenched and then my pulse took flight on the wings of the irrational hope that someone was coming to tell me there'd been a mistake, that Obligate Belinda was alive and well and ready to go to Calisto.

Mother answered the door, and though I could see from my position near the fireplace that she tried hard to stay composed, a tiny gasp slipped out before she pressed her fingers to her mouth.

I went to her side to find a boy—the same one who'd come to tell Mr. Arsen that Belinda was dead—holding up an old sack on a hanger. Except it wasn't a sack, I realized as I looked down and saw a swath of black fabric peeking out from the lower edge. It was the dress I would wear to Calisto.

I reached for it, vaguely wondering if we were supposed to tip the boy and then deciding it wasn't important.

Mother closed the door while I turned to take the dress to my bedroom, walking carefully and holding it away from me as if it were a dead rat that might suddenly reanimate and snap at me.

In my room, I took a deep breath and then pulled the sack off the dress. I dropped the sack, placed the hanger on a hook near the door, and stepped back.

My pulse throbbed in my temples as I looked at the dress. It was identical to the wrinkled and dusty white Obligate Elect dress that I still wore, except it was a black so deep it seemed to absorb and obliterate the faint light in the room. A stark white cord was slung around the neck of the hanger. White—blank—to signify that I would no longer be part of a clan.

The dress had been made for Belinda, but it looked as if it should fit me well enough. We were about the same build, though she was a couple of inches taller than me if I remembered correctly.

I'd turned my back on the dress with a shudder.

Later, as I sat with Mother and Lana among our neighbors who were enjoying the feast, the black dress still hung in my room. I wouldn't have to put it on until the afternoon. Instead, I wore my favorite dress—a short, lightweight shift in a delicate robin's egg blue, a color that contrasted nicely with my hair, which was the dark brown color of a cacao bar.

Occasionally someone came to place a hand on my shoulder and offer a murmured prayer of strength or gratitude. Every time it happened, Mother stiffened. I'd kept an eye out for Rand but didn't see him or his parents.

I watched children chasing after each other with food in their hands, laughing and shouting and staining their clothes on the grass. A few boys knelt in the dirt, drawing shapes with sticks in a game I vaguely remembered. Would any of them grow up to be Obligates, someday sitting in my place with their mourning but brave-faced families?

After an hour or two had passed and I hadn't managed to eat a single bite from the plate in front of me, Lana leaned close to Mother. "Can we go home?"

My twin looked as exhausted as I felt, and Mother's face seemed to have aged a decade since yesterday morning. Mother nodded, and we rose from the table, one of many pulled from nearby houses into the small courtyard in our neighborhood.

Just as we turned toward our end of the neighborhood, I caught a glimpse of a familiar face. "I'll be right back, I need to speak to someone," I said to Mother and Lana, my eyes on the muscular young man who was walking alone. It was Orion.

Without waiting for their responses, I left them at a quick walk, not wanting to lose Orion in the crowd.

When I caught up to him and touched his arm, he started and whipped his head toward me, his piercing, pale blue eyes guarded. I didn't realize he'd been so deep in thought, and I felt a twinge of guilt for disrupting him.

I pulled my hand back and retreated half a step. "I'm sorry, I didn't mean to startle you, Orion. I just wanted to tell you, well, I actually just wanted to say thank you." I took a breath, trying to compose myself under his steady gaze. "You came to my aid during the Selection in a way that was kind and profoundly generous considering what you were going through yourself."

I fidgeted, tweaking the fabric of my dress between my fingers. I suddenly wanted an excuse to talk with Orion, or at least walk with him a bit. He was one of the only people on Earthenfell who understood what was going through my mind and heart. And he'd brought me a shred of comfort in what was the worst moment of my life. Even though we'd never really known each other, our situation gave us a connection, and I suddenly felt as if surviving the rest of the day depended on acknowledging it.

"I'm pleased I could do something for you, though I think you're giving me more credit than I'm due." His eyes softened, the guarded look from a moment before fading. His voice was quiet but resonant, the type of voice that made people want to listen precisely because it didn't demand attention. "How are your mother and sister coping?"

I gave him a tiny, grateful smile for acknowledging how difficult the day was for my family. Then I shook my head and closed my eyes for a brief moment. "They're being very brave. But . . ." I trailed off and shook my head again. "What about your family?"

He drew a heavy breath. "My parents are quite devastated. I have no siblings," he said simply.

His frank way of speaking was such a relief, and it seemed to cut free some of the heaviness dragging at my heart.

"And you?" I asked softly. "How are you doing?"

He pressed his lips together and his eyes went distant for the briefest of moments, and then he focused back on me. "I will face what's ahead, and I will throw myself into what I must do to survive. But I worry about my parents. I have something to focus on. But they face only the emptiness of my absence."

I stared at him in awed silence, my lips parted.

They face only the emptiness of my absence.

Orion was much too eloquent to have been stuck in machinery. Not that he had to worry about his job on Earthenfell anymore. "I'm sure your strength is giving them strength," I said.

His shoulders relaxed in a subtle shift. "Thank you for that."

I sensed that he needed to be on his way, probably to his family as I needed to get back to mine.

"Would it be okay if I look for you later? At the Departure?" My stomach churned at the mere mention of leaving Earthenfell and also at making such a request of someone who was practically a stranger.

His eyes warmed. "Yes, I would like that." He said it as if we'd make plans to walk through the orchards together at dusk, and I tried to hold on to that thought.

He lifted his hand in a little wave and then turned and tucked his chin against his chest, already back in his own thoughts, as he strode away.

I turned toward my own neighborhood and set off at a quick pace, hoping to catch up with Mother and Lana. For some reason, the thought of them arriving home without me tore at my heart. One last time, we should all go home from Feast Day together.

When I saw them up ahead, strolling with their arms linked, my breath rushed out in relief. I caught up to them and went to Lana's other side. My hand found the crook of her elbow.

They both turned to me, curiosity on their faces.

"Orion was so good to me before. I just had to tell him thank you," I said. I brightened as an idea came to me. "Do you think you could do something for me after I'm gone?"

My heart dipped as I heard myself say the word. *Gone.* But I was trying to follow Orion's example, trying to be frank about it.

"Of course," Lana said.

"Anything," Mother echoed.

"I think it would be nice if you could visit Orion's parents. He has no brothers or sisters. I think, well, I think they might find comfort in your company. Or maybe not, I don't really know them. Perhaps I shouldn't presume . . ." I trailed off, suddenly uncertain.

"No, I'd like that," Lana said.

Mother nodded, and a faint smile passed over her face. The energy between the three of us seemed to lighten. It took me a moment to realize that my suggestion had given them something to focus on. *Purpose.* It was so important to feel a sense of purpose.

What had my purpose been, before the Selection? My life before felt like a faded, years-old memory. Before the Selection, my purpose had been Court. Yes, marrying Court and living my dream of a future with him.

In the space of a day, I was losing Court, my family, my life on Earthenfell, and my future.

One of the things that cut deepest was the knowledge that being an Obligate meant I'd lost any control over the path of my life right when I was on the verge of being able to make meaningful decisions about what kind of life I wanted. I no longer had the freedom to choose a husband, create a home of my own, or have a family.

I turned my eyes to the sky, and my gaze hardened. My new purpose would be survival, proving myself to Lord Toric so that he would take me into his harem. But I didn't want only to survive. I would find a way to gain some sort of freedom. There was no point in surviving if I had no control over my own life. I *would* find a way.

I STARED INTO the wide eyes of the black-clad young woman in Mother's narrow mirror, my stomach gripped into a tight ball. It still did not quite seem real. How could that be me? How could I be standing in Mother's room, wearing Departure black and readying myself to leave Earthenfell for Calisto?

Obligate Maya. That's what the people offering me prayers throughout Feast Day had called me. Every time, the phrase had dropped like a weight into my ears. Every time, I had the urge to turn and say, "You've made a mistake. Obligate Belinda is the one you're looking for."

But Belinda was dead, and I was wearing her black dress and her white cord looped around my waist. As I'd expected, the hem of the dress dragged too long on the floor. I'd have to walk carefully, perhaps gather the fabric in my hands and hold it up to keep from tripping.

It was odd to think that her family had been preparing to lose her for months, years. But instead of passing through the portal to Calisto with the other fifteen Obligates, Belinda would remain on Earthenfell, but gone from life. I'd heard she would be buried the next day.

Part of me wondered: was Belinda's fate preferable to mine? Only nineteen years of life, but at least she didn't die in a strange alien land.

There was a rap at the door.

"Maya?" Lana's soft voice interrupted my macabre thoughts, and I was relieved to have the distraction.

"Come in."

I took a deep breath and turned from the mirror. Mother stared at me, her mouth pinched and her eyes squinting. Lana couldn't see me, of course, but pain was so clear in her eyes it made it feel as though she could.

I suddenly hated that Mother's last memory of me was the image of a pale-faced girl clad in black Departure garb. In a dead girl's dress.

I knew it was time to go, but my feet were rooted to where I stood, refusing to take a step.

Lana left Mother's side and moved to me. She felt for my hand and wrapped her fingers tightly around mine. Only with her hand gripping mine was I able to unstick my feet and force myself move. She led me out of Mother's bedroom, through the living room, and to the front door. There, she stopped and half-turned her head, listening for Mother behind us.

Lana felt for the doorknob, opened the door, and walked outside ahead of me with her hand still firm around mine.

I held my breath as I passed through the doorway, trying to numb my heart to the knowledge that I would never pass through it again. I kept my body rigid, refusing to look over my shoulder to watch Mother close the door.

Lana let go of my hand to link her elbow with mine, pressing close to my side as if huddling against a frigid winter wind. Mother took my other elbow.

I forced my face into a neutral mask and locked my eyes on the ground a few feet ahead of us. It was half an hour from sunset and the low-angled dwindling light of the sun made our shadows stretch out in a diagonal in front of us. Three walking shadows pulling ahead and to our left, as if trying to coax us to turn that way.

But that wasn't where we were headed. I lifted my eyes to the horizon and trained them onto the gentle V between two low foothills. At the base of that V, the overlords would open the portal to Calisto.

A shock of worry shot through me. Would Mother be able to walk all the way to the portal? Perhaps I should have asked Rand if his father could take her in their car.

But her footsteps kept up with mine and Lana's, and her breaths were quiet and even with no hint of wheezing. The walk, unlike the steep path up to the pavilion, was over nearly level ground. I sensed that she needed to make it on the power of her own two feet, so I let that worry slip away.

I heard the shuffle of shoes all around us, the murmur of low voices, but didn't care to look around or identify anyone nearby. The only people who mattered at all were the two at my sides.

I lowered my eyelids for a moment, trying to take in the sensations of the cooling evening breeze, the earthy scent of alfalfa harvested from a nearby field, the way the dry ground gritted under my shoes. The exact *feel* of being on Earthenfell.

I opened my eyes to the deepening colors of the sunset. Would there be a sunset on Calisto? If there were, would I ever be allowed to watch it?

"I will write you, as often as I'm allowed," Lana said, and I started at the sound of her voice.

I tipped my head toward hers, and we leaned into each other for a moment. "Thank you," I whispered. I'd forgotten that letters could be sent from Earthenfell to the departed Obligates. But I would not be permitted to write back.

The voices and sounds of movement around us thickened as we neared the site of the portal, and I finally glanced around. The faces around me were familiar yet strange, as if my mind were already trying to condition me to the idea that soon I would no longer be one of them.

The crowd slowed, and we slowed with it. I gave myself a mental shake, remembering that I could not hang back as I had six months ago, six months before that, twice a year for as long as I could recall. I forced my feet forward. Mother, Lana, and I threaded through the throng as I aimed us at the point of the V between hills that had looked like gently rolling bumps from a distance but closer up loomed tall enough to blot out much of the sky.

The crowd parted as people turned and saw me in my black dress. A few touched my shoulder or offered a quick word of praise.

At the front edge of the crowd, I stopped. A very old concrete bridge with two crumbling levels and exposed girders joined the two sides of the ravine.

During the spring rains, the ravine filled with water that rushed to meet the river that flowed along the edge of town. At the spring Departure six months ago, when I'd stood back in the crowd as the Obligates passed over the bridge, the rushing sound of the water had added a majestic element to the ceremony. But in the fall season, the ravine was only a darkened muddy line cutting through the hills.

The Selection Controller, again with her hair in a neat gray-streaked bun, stood on the ground near the bridge. She took something from the pocket of her dress—a timepiece—and glanced at it.

The low murmurs in the crowd began to fade. Mother's arm was trembling against mine. I found her hand and held it tightly. On my other side, Lana drew herself up tall and took a deep breath.

On the edge of my vision, I saw someone's face turned toward me and felt the weight of a gaze. I looked past Lana to see Rand standing solemnly with his arms in front of him, one hand clasped over the back of the other as if he were about to bow his head in prayer.

His eyes seemed to burn into mine, and his lips trembled. When I realized he was on the verge of tears, I quickly looked away, focusing on the Selection Controller. As when he'd left me late last night, an uneasy sensation twisted through my stomach, perhaps lingering guilt that I did not feel for him what he felt for me.

The Controller raised one arm above her head, signaling for quiet. "The sun has set and the time has come for the Obligates to begin their service. Obligates, please approach."

There was some shifting as young black-clad men and women separated themselves from the crowd. I sucked in a ragged breath as my hands gripped Lana's and my mother's so hard I must have hurt them. But they did not wince or try to pull away.

It was time.

I let go, turned to Mother, and folded my arms around her thin shoulders.

"Never forget how dearly I love you, Maya," she whispered.

"I love you too, Mother." I choked out the words, my mouth against her hair. I wanted to say more, but all the words in the universe would fall short of what was truly in my heart.

I turned to Lana. "My twin, my other half," I said, my

cheek pressing against her wet one. "Be strong and know that I'm always with you."

"I'm *always* with you," Lana said fiercely. "I love you, dear sister, as much as a human heart can love."

"I love you, too."

And then I let go, turned my back to them, and went to join the other Obligates.

I couldn't breathe. My lungs felt stuffed with wadded paper, my throat too tight to allow air to pass through. The other Obligates were forming a half-circle around the Controller. Someone gently bumped my right elbow, and I looked over, dazed.

Orion nodded at me. I nodded back, and my chest loosened enough to draw a trembling breath.

The sixteen Earth Bearers who had been waiting off to the side filed into the half circle, one standing in front of each of us. They held simple glass jars filled with rich brown soil. In unison, they stretched out their arms, presenting the jars to us.

I grasped my jar in both hands, gripping hard to try to stop the quaking of my arms. The Controller was reciting the short rite about the jars of soil, the offerings we would take to the overlords on Calisto.

And then the Controller was leading us up a short, worn path to the edge of the lower level of the bridge. She stopped and pointed, indicating the first Obligate in line, a short young man, should keep walking across the bridge.

My eyes blurred and I blinked tears away. Clutching

my jar—the only thing I was allowed to take with me from Earthenfell besides the clothes I wore and the nearly twenty years of memories of my life there—I followed the Obligate in front of me.

Ahead, the shimmering light of the portal, like sunlight kissing a wind-dappled pond, beckoned us to Calisto.

7

Toric

I WENT OUT to my widest balcony just as the larger of Calisto's two suns winked its last light over the edge of the horizon and dipped out of sight. This balcony adjoined my bed chamber and overlooked my family's private gardens, which were filled with exquisite replicas of old Earth trees and flowering plants. Beyond the garden wall, I could see the portal pad where the young Earthens—the Offered—would come from Earthenfell.

As soon as I saw movement at the portal, I honed my focus there. Earlier, I'd been informed that this offering of Earthens included ten women and six men.

The first figure through the portal was a young man, short and with flopping brown hair. Even from a distance, I could sense his anxiety and doubt. The next was a woman with voluptuous curves and blonde ringlets that bounced around her shoulders. She emanated determination, and I would have bet my finest silk robe that she was one of those who had received training, an Offered who had long been pre-selected by her clan. Then there was another young woman, petite with dark olive skin and medium brown hair whose energy was drawn tight like the strings of a mandola. She was unremarkable except that I sensed she was innocent—a virgin.

The fourth Offered through the portal drew my attention before my eyes even had a chance to focus on her. My breath caught in my throat.

Her energy was . . . fascinating. Complex. It was fractured, turbulent, and danced on the surface of her being as if unaware of the great depth of space it could explore. Like a fish that swam only in the top few inches of the sea, oblivious to the vast caves, reefs, delicacies, and dangers that existed below.

This woman with her raven waves of hair, straight back, and stoic expression possessed an energy unlike any of the dozens of Earthenfell women I'd encountered in the years since I'd ascended to the Lordship. I didn't know yet what it meant, but it made my pulse race. She was also an innocent, but her energy was not completely innocent—there was a dark edge to it, something I suspected she herself wasn't even aware of.

She was a study in contrasts. A heavenly being, but with a reservoir of darkness. An innocent with a deep capacity for seduction. A slave girl who was filled with purpose. I'd never sensed so much about an Earthen Offered, never in so much detail.

A dark angel.

That was the image her energy brought to my mind.

The old Earth religion of angels and demons, Heaven and Hell, God above and Devil below, had faded from practice many centuries back, but part of my spiritual training had included its texts. The parts about the angels had always captivated me.

I tried to examine the other Offered coming through, but my eyes kept going back to the dark-haired woman. I wished I could see her up close, read what was in her eyes.

My fingers clenched around the railing of the balcony. I would formally receive the Earthen Offered soon, after they got their implants, but that was hours away. I needed to feel this young woman's energy up close. The throbbing of desire deep in my core seemed to urge me on.

I whirled and hurried back into my chambers, and then stopped short at the sight of Victor, my primary servant. He was smoothing fresh cotton sheets over my bed, the rumpled ones from my afternoon tryst—this time with gentle Mee-Young, as I'd temporarily sought reprieve from Sytoria's whips—piled on the floor. His back was to me and he gave no indication that he'd heard me come in, though I suspected he was perfectly aware that I stood here. This was one of the things that had earned him the position of primary among my personal servants—not only did he anticipate my needs as if he could read my mind, he knew when to look away or to give me a moment to collect myself.

I went to the carved teakwood cart where the linen curtains on one side of the balcony billowed in the breeze that swept in through the open balcony doors. I poured myself a tumbler of ginger lily and bergamine-infused water and then set the pitcher down noisily on purpose.

As I sipped, I angled my body away from Victor so he couldn't see that I was partially aroused. I wasn't hiding out of modesty. For some reason, I didn't want him—or anyone—to know how strongly the dark angel's energy had affected me.

"May I fetch something, or perhaps someone, for you, my Lord?"

I looked over my shoulder. Victor stood at the foot of my made bed, the dirty linens gathered in his arms.

"I need nothing at the moment," I said. "I'll be going out soon."

Victor inclined his head and turned to go.

"Ah, one thing," I said. He paused at the door, waiting. I pretended to think for a moment. "Have Darafina waiting for my return."

He inclined his head again, his expression remaining studiously neutral, and then slipped from my bed chamber and closed the door behind him.

I'd tried to make it sound as if I'd picked Darafina on a whim, but out of all the women in my harem, she was the only one with hair nearly the color of the dark angel's. I'd never been particularly attracted to Darafina before, but now the thought of her hair spread out over the crisp linens on the pillows . . .

I set down my tumbler and planted my hands on the cart, leaning heavily enough to make it creak under my weight. Flashes of memories from my imprisonment suddenly tore through my mind. I gritted my teeth and groaned, remembering, as I had a million times before, the way my captors had forced torment and pleasure, pain and release, to mingle together in my body, my mind, my soul.

Blood pounded in my veins as I tried to breathe through the torrent of images and the force of my own unwanted desire. I focused instead on the dark angel. The golden skin of her face and bare arms. Her shining hair that nearly blended with the black dress she wore. The set of her chin, and the way her slender fingers held the offering jar.

To my deep relief and gratitude, those thoughts soothed the terrible images from my mind. My arousal was even stronger than before, but for once my mind was free of torment.

I straightened, tipped my head back, and breathed deeply, relishing in the rare experience of pure, untainted desire.

WHEN I LEFT my chambers, I tried to keep to the lesser-used passages of the palace, even taking some of the service hallways to avoid running into councilors, nobles, or others who might want to stop me for a word. Most of all, I wanted to avoid Jeric.

I wasn't completely sure of the location of the servants' medical facility and took a few wrong turns. Most of the servants I encountered had the grace to quickly stop and bow when they recognized me, averting their questioning glances.

The humid smell of soapy water and clean linens told me when I was near the palace laundry. Laughter and cheery chatter rang out freely from the washrooms. I slowed, enjoying the sounds of the women inside. When the workers caught sight of me, they silenced, their hands stilled, and they all curtsied. One of them, a young woman who looked barely old enough to hold such a position, peeked up at me from under her eyelashes and hid her face when she realized I was looking straight at her.

I kept on, but almost wished I could pause to eavesdrop on their conversation. I never truly knew what the people of Calisto thought of me. There were plenty of rumors that I was some sort of sexual deviant. The rumors would not have come from the Earthenfell women in my harem nor from the Earthenfell men who were my personal servants—their spinal implants ensured that—but everyone on Calisto knew of my abduction and something of the nature of my torture while I was in enemy hands.

The guards who stood outside the doors of my chambers were military-trained Calistans, as were the two guards who trailed me even now. Perhaps the guards spread rumors about me. It was odd to think that the Earthens who served here in the palace were likely the most loyal of all the servants due to their implants. If Calistans had implants, how many of them would be exposed as traitors or gossip mongers?

Again, I thought of my brother.

When I finally reached the servants' medical facility, I realized I had no idea exactly what I would do next. I turned to the two bodyguards who had tailed me.

"Palovich," I said, beckoning to the taller of the two guards. "Please inform the head of surgery that I wish to survey the new arrivals as soon as they are all in recovery."

"Yes, my Lord."

As soon as I said it, it sank in how unorthodox my request would appear, and how it could easily be used to fuel more rumors of my oddities. But Palovich was already through the doors.

The other guard, Calvin, swept his gaze around the bare portico, alert for any movement or sound. When one of the doors to the clinic swung outward, his posture didn't change but his hand twitched on the side where his dagger and gun were holstered. A young Calistan woman, presumably a palace servant, towing a wide-eyed child of about three or four years old emerged. The woman flicked a pleasant smile my way and then stopped short with a double-take and curtsied, her chin pressed to her chest.

"My Lord," she said and then raised her head. I nodded absently and looked away at a point in the distance. Over the years I'd discovered it was best to remain aloof with Calistan commoners. It was what they expected of their Lord, and it was simply easier to fulfill their expectation.

"Perhaps you'd prefer to wait over here," Calvin said to me, gesturing to a replica of a rambling hedge at the corner of the facility. He went ahead of me to check around the corner and then nodded. "It's clear."

Feeling more than a little foolish, I concealed myself behind the fake plant where passersby wouldn't seem me while Calvin watched for Palovich. As the minutes passed, I began to think that I'd made a mistake, that I should have just mustered the patience to wait until I formally received the new Offered.

Finally, Palovich returned. "My Lord, the Offered have their implants and are now in a recovery room." He led me to the door and held it for me, and Calvin followed. "According to the head of surgery, they will be unconscious for another thirty minutes. He will take you to them."

A distinguished-looking, reedy man in the tight-fitting white clothing of medical professionals waited for us in front of an empty reception counter. The waiting room was also vacant of patients. I felt a twinge of self-reproach at my early suspicions of the guards and my assumptions that they contributed to Calisto's rumor mill. I'd have to remember to praise Palovich later for making sure the way was clear for my entry.

Without introducing himself, the doctor simply bowed and then turned to take us through the empty hallways. I suspected his cool demeanor was meant to express his disapproval of my visit or misgivings about my intentions with the Offered.

When he stopped outside a closed door, my pulse quickened. The dark angel was on the other side.

"Doctor," I said. "Would you be so kind as to accompany me and describe the recovery process?"

The doctor blinked rapidly a couple of times, and then his expression relaxed a bit. "Of course, my Lord."

I was almost certain I'd guessed his thoughts. He'd expected me to want time alone with the unconscious Offered.

Palovich and Calvin stationed themselves on either side of the door while I followed the doctor inside. I took in a slow breath, trying to calm the nervous anticipation that fluttered through my chest.

The room was long and narrow, with hospital beds set in a row across one of the long walls and heavy transparent plastic curtains separating the beds. The energies of the Offered were subdued, dampened by the medication that kept them asleep while they recovered. But I could already feel distinct tendrils of the dark angel's energy rising above the background hum of the others. It was like a delicious aroma carried on an otherwise ordinary summer breeze.

The doctor and I walked slowly past the foot of each bed as he described the procedure for inserting the spinal implant at the base of the skull and the recovery, which was less a healing from the implant itself and more a chance for the neurons of the spine to rearrange and join properly with the device.

I half-listened and nodded every so often, but my eyes were glued to the still figures under the white sheets.

I felt the energy of the dark angel, giving me her precise location, before I reached her bed. And just before I came to her, I noticed the names displayed on the small screens attached to the foot of each bed. We passed a muscular young man with handsome, angular features. His screen identified him as Orion.

Next was the dark angel. I wanted to know her name, but when I stepped into the space that allowed me a view of her, I couldn't seem to tear my eyes from her face.

I tried to absorb every detail. Her dark hair fanned out around her head and shoulders, contrasting sharply with the white pillowcase. Brows a slight shade lighter than her hair framed her eyes in subtle arches. Her nose was delicate and a bit narrower than what would be considered ideal, but somehow balanced with her other features—lower lip a bit fuller than the upper, slight hollows under her cheekbones, small ears. Even with the stress of her departure from her home world and the implant procedure she'd just undergone, her skin glowed with vitality. It had a subtle golden quality, naturally sunkissed.

The doctor was still talking, but I was transfixed.

The dark angel's lashes stirred as her eyes moved under her eyelids. I held my breath as her eyelids slowly opened. Her energy swelled in a crescendo and thundered into me, a heady tidal wave. For a moment that seemed to stretch out and yet end all too soon, her blue-gray eyes met mine. Then her lids lowered and her energy quieted, as if I'd imagined the last few seconds.

"Doctor, should the patients be waking up so soon?" I

asked in a hushed tone.

I glanced at him as he raised his brows in surprise. "Not for several more minutes at least." He looked up at the monitors mounted over the dark angel's bed. "This one is still under. If any were waking too soon, an alarm would sound."

I nodded, but I was sure of what I'd seen. Just before we moved on to the next bed, I remembered to glance down at the dark angel's screen.

Maya.

Her name was Maya.

8

Maya

PASSING THROUGH THE portal that connected Earthenfell to Calisto was like walking through some strange underwater dream-window. The light of the portal had a physical quality to it, seeming to cling to my skin like a thick mist. When it grew painfully bright, I squeezed my eyelids closed, trusting that my feet would find solid ground as I continued to move forward.

I knew when I'd passed through because the air of Calisto felt immediately foreign. It was lighter, thinner somehow, and much drier than I was accustomed to. And it was empty of anything reminiscent of home. No scent of harvest or chimney smoke. No weight of decaying autumn foliage. Not even a whiff of trash, sewage, or other human-generated smells.

When I opened my eyes and blinked away the spots left

by the bright light of the portal, the first thing I saw was a thin sliver of red-orange light disappearing over the horizon. I inhaled and my heart lifted as sudden emotion swelled in my chest. There *were* sunsets on Calisto. I gasped again when I realized there was another disc of light in the sky, a small yellow-orange sun still shining.

Two suns. My sorrows muted for a moment as I marveled at the wonder.

"You have arrived on Calisto," pronounced a voice in a lilting accent.

My head whipped to a woman who stood at least half a foot taller than me. Her eyes were wide-set and hooded, and her skin the gray-taupe color of the Earthen foothills in late autumn. She was the first Calistan I'd ever seen, and I couldn't help but stare. I'd imagined Calistans to look more . . . alien. She did look exotic to me, but not quite as strange as I'd expected.

I silently chided myself. Even children knew that the Calistans were distant biological relatives of the natives of Earthenfell. Calistans were "alien" because they'd lived away from Earthenfell for many thousands of years, and we had evolved separately from them. On the outside we were obviously different from each other in some ways, but I knew from what I'd learned in school that genetically Calistans and Earthens were very close to identical. After all, we'd both descended from the same ancient Earthen ancestors.

The woman surveyed us coolly, her upper lip curling. "I am Akantha, Mistress of Tournament. Do not address any

Calistan unless I give you permission to do so. Follow me."
She flipped a beckoning finger at the first Obligate in line.

I watched the Mistress of Tournament, fascinated. The
way she moved was subtly different than Earthens. Her gait
seemed more sinuous and graceful, with her long limbs and
slender neck giving her the quality of a dancer.

But there was something sharp about her conduct toward
us. Even after only a glance and a few spoken words, it was
clear she found it distasteful to be dealing with us. And that
she offered no explanation about what was next just added to
my tension. I gripped the jar of soil as if it held my own beating
heart, trying to see ahead to guess where she was leading us.

We filed along a wall with trees peeking over the top of it. It
seemed to be late spring on Calisto, by the verdant appearance
of the trees. Assuming that Calisto had seasons as we had on
Earthenfell, anyway.

When my gaze rose above the trees, my breath caught. The
dark angular structure beyond had to be the palace. Lord Toric
was somewhere up there.

The palace was beautiful, in a foreboding way. It was
constructed of some sort of smooth material the color of
gray-black slate. Narrow towers—or perhaps just decorative
spires—knifed upward into the reddish-purple Calistan sky.

Movement on a high balcony of the palace caught my eye.
The breeze was stirring curtains on either side of the balcony,
and a lone figure stood at the railing. It was too far for me
to make out details, but the figure appeared to be a Calistan

man. A curious tremor, a frosty-hot sensation, vibrated up and down my body. I shivered as my heart thumped harder in my chest.

"Maya, keep walking," Orion whispered behind me, and I jumped, not realizing I'd slowed enough to allow a large gap to grow between me and the Obligate ahead.

I took a few running steps to catch up. Akantha was taking us into a portico, a walkway with a domed roof and open sides sectioned by slender columns. When I lost sight of the palace, I felt a faint tug of disappointment.

As we toured through more covered walkways, we encountered several Calistans, and I couldn't help staring at them. Even the shortest Calistan was taller than all of us Obligates. Their skin colors ranged the spectrum of grays and browns, from the delicate gray of an Earthenfell cloud to a dark umber nearly the same color as the rich soil in my jar.

Every Calistan we passed bowed his or her head at Akantha, but she did not bow in return.

Just as we reached a smooth gray door set into the side of a slick-looking windowless building, it struck me that the only natural things we had encountered were the trees over the wall. The ground we walked on was a pebbly-looking brown rubber surface that at first glance I had assumed was dirt, but it was some sort of artificial flooring. I lifted my jar and inhaled the scent of soil. It was such a potent reminder of home, and I had to swallow back tears.

Thoughts of Earthenfell rushed to the forefront of my

mind. What were Mother and Lana doing? Were they back at home yet? How would Lana fare without me when work in the orchard resumed on Monday?

I pulled my lips in between my teeth and bit down hard, trying to steel myself against the tide of emotions rising up. I forced myself to look around, to focus on my surroundings.

We'd entered some sort of facility with white plastic-looking walls lining the hallways and a smooth floor made of slightly springy gray-and-white mottled tiles.

In the stupor of grief at leaving home and the disorientation of passing through the portal, I'd failed to truly consider what would come next, and the space offered almost no clues.

When we passed a pair of Calistan women, they leaned toward each other and whispered. When their eyes fell to the jar in my hands, their expressions shifted from curiosity to a sort of hungry awe.

I turned my head to one side to whisper over my shoulder to Orion, "Where are we going?"

A sheen of cold sweat slicked my palms as we came upon a group of four Calistans dressed in tight-fitting white clothing. They stared intently at each of us and equally intently at our jars.

"I don't know," Orion said. "Maybe a medical exam?"

If we were in some sort of medical facility, it was nothing like the neighborhood clinics we had on Earthenfell.

Akantha turned and stopped, pinning me with a hard look. "Do not speak to each other unless I've given you permission to do so. This is the last warning you will get, and it goes for all of you. If you'd like to test me, it would be my pleasure to demonstrate your punishment."

She brandished a stubby metal wand. When she pressed a button on it, the end of it glowed white hot and a blue arc of electricity bowed outward. I drew back and clamped my elbows to my sides, not daring to breathe until she put the wand away.

Akantha took us around a left turn that dead-ended at a door. She gestured to a cabinet next to the door. "Place your vessels in here."

Though Akantha had not yet treated us with any particular cruelty, she clearly had no qualms about ordering us around and treating us like annoying wayward children. I'd always wondered how the overlords would address and treat Earthens. We were their servants—slaves—both here on Calisto and back on Earthenfell. We worked the land of Earthenfell to keep it fertile for when the Calistan Lord, either the current Lord Toric or some future Lord, would lead his people back to Earthenfell and reclaim their ancestral home. And we supplied the Calistans with food and a wide variety of goods.

I had no idea if Akantha's treatment of us was better, worse, or typical of how we'd be treated by other Calistans. My stomach tightened into a hard ball. I suspected that worse was yet to come, but the most difficult part was simply not knowing what awaited us.

As we obediently placed our jars on the shelves of the cabinet I glanced at the other Obligates. I knew a few of them by name, and recognized most of their faces from when I was still in school. Orion was the only one I'd spoken to recently. I would need to become familiar with all of them. They would be—they already *were*—my competition.

Akantha opened the door, revealing a long room with plastic curtains dividing narrow beds made up with plain white linens. "Choose a bed and lie down. Do as you are asked by the medics."

I went to one of the beds toward the middle, and Orion took one right next to me. The plastic curtains allowed light through but distorted what was one the other side.

My heart tapped a rapid nervous rhythm as I fidgeted with the folds of my dress.

I heard the door open again, and then the shuffle of many pairs of feet entering. Calistans dressed like the ones we'd seen in the hallways walked passed the foot of my bed. One, a man with light taupe skin and a shock of short black hair, stopped when he reached me.

He held a small, flat monitor and a pointed object that was mostly concealed in his large hand. Extending the monitor toward me, he said, "Speak your name."

I did as he asked.

He attached the monitor to the foot of my bed and came around to my right side. "Sit up and tip your head down. Hold still."

I caught a glimpse of the object in his hand. It had a wickedly sharp tapered end. When he raised it, I sucked in a gasp, suddenly realizing what it was.

An implant, like the ones the man who weighed our collection bags and the woman who directed the Selection had at the backs of their necks.

I started to shake my head and tried to lean away, but the medic's hands were lightning fast. He wrapped his fingers around the side of my neck, and a sharp prick of pain zapped between my shoulder blades and zipped the length of my spine.

My entire body seemed to melt, my muscles softening, and my nerves numbing. There was a soft click and an impact that pushed my upper body forward like I'd been rammed from behind, and then I was falling.

Falling . . . back to the pillow at the head of the bed. My brain swam in a dizzy swirl, and eons seemed to pass before the back of my head finally contacted with the pillow.

My eyelids closed, blotting out the world.

A moment later—or maybe it was an hour, I had no idea—I heard voices. Male voices, I thought. Definitely Calistan accents.

My eyelids seemed to weigh a hundred pounds apiece, but they wanted to open. I couldn't move my limbs or even feel much of anything, but my eyes wanted to see who was talking nearby while I drifted.

At first I saw only bright light. From the light, two figures took shape. One was talking, but I was not interested in him.

The other was looking right at me, his blue-green eyes so intent, as if he were trying to absorb me through his gaze.

It was him.

I don't know how I knew, but I was sure: this was the man who'd been standing on the balcony when I'd first stepped onto Calisto.

I wanted to pour myself into those exotic eyes, but my eyelids grew too heavy. My senses numbed again, those mesmerizing eyes and the voices fading away.

THE THROBBING AT the back of my neck was the first thing I became aware of when I awoke again. The remnants of a dream, of aquamarine eyes, tried to solidify in my mind, but slipped and faded away before I could clearly recall it.

The muscles of my neck and back cramped, and I froze with a groan. Through clenched teeth, I breathed into the spasms, and once they passed, I moved more cautiously.

The sighs and groans nearby told me that the other Obligates were rousing, too.

I raised a tentative hand to the back of my neck and brushed it with my fingertips. I winced at the feel of the metal disc, but there was no pain. Just the throbbing, which I'd at first taken for the throb of a swelling wound but now realized it was a faint pulse at the site of the implant, in sync with the rhythm of my heartbeat.

The rest of my body felt different, too. A silent buzz seemed to reverberate in every cell. My attention was somehow sharper. Heightened. No, it was my senses that were more aware.

I felt more *alive*. As if I could feel my own blood singing through my vessels, feel on the air the night-black of the dress I wore and the bleached white of the sheet against my bare arm, sense the radiance of every object and person in the room.

My heart pounded as I tried to take it all in.

"Rise and move to the foot of your bed," came Akantha's voice from somewhere in the room.

I did as she commanded and drew slow breaths, trying to calm my pulse. Looking back and forth, I saw stunned faces with wide eyes. More than anything, I wanted to ask the purpose of the implants in our necks. On Earthenfell, we'd been told only that Earthens who had implants, who worked directly for the overlords, needed the implants for communication. My eyes widened in apprehension. Could the Calistans read our thoughts through our implants?

I turned to Orion and our eyes met. I raised my brows, and he responded with a slight dazed shake of his head.

"You will be allowed a brief meal and break to use the facilities, and then Lord Toric will receive you at your formal introductions," Akantha said.

Finally, a clue about what to expect. I looked down at my rumpled black dress and tried to smooth the creases across my stomach. Would we at least get fresh clothes to go before the alien Lord?

Back in the hallway, Akantha opened the cabinet and nodded at it. "Retrieve your vessels."

A curvy Obligate with waves of golden-blonde hair pinned up behind her ears appeared to be trying to get Orion's attention. She moved close to him and bumped him with her elbow a couple of times. When Akantha's back was turned to secure the door of the room we'd just exited, the girl stood on tiptoe to whisper in his ear. Kalindi was her name, if my memory was correct.

Orion looked down at her in question, and then cast a furtive glance at Akantha. He seemed about to respond to Kalindi when Akantha finished with the door and looked down, reaching for something in her pocket.

Another female Obligate, a lithe young woman with a sprinkling of freckles across her button nose and stylish bobbed hair the color of sherry wine, had also been trying to catch the eye of one of the male Obligates. That young man had the same muscular build as Orion. Perhaps they'd both come from machinery.

Others had also been shifting and jockeying while Akantha's attention was elsewhere, I realized.

Unease crept through me like a chilly morning mist. I wasn't quite sure what was going on among some of the Obligates, but I got the distinct impression that it was something I needed to decipher.

The freckled Obligate didn't seem to notice that Akantha had turned her attention toward us. The girl pulled at the young man's arm and gave him an imploring look. The first part of what she said was lost in the rustle of shoes and clothing, but I distinctly heard, ". . . to work together as a pair."

She might have gotten away with it if the hallway had not gone silent just as she'd finished whispering.

Akantha narrowed her eyes as she stalked to the girl. When the Calistan whipped out her hand, I thought it was to strike the Obligate. Instead, she grabbed the girl's wrist and pressed her short wand against the girl's arm.

The Obligate screamed and writhed, trying to yank her arm away. Akantha held the wand to the girl's arm for a couple of seconds and then let go, and the Obligate stumbled backward, crashed into the wall, and fell in a heap to the floor. She moaned in agony, holding her arm.

"Let the others see," Akantha commanded.

Gasping, the girl stared at Akantha as if she didn't understand.

"You." Akantha turned her gaze on me. "Make her stand and hold out her arm."

I gulped, hurried to the wall, and hauled the girl to her feet. Her chest was heaving, though she managed to hold back tears. I gently peeled her fingers away and unfolded the arm she had clutched to her stomach.

When I saw the angry wound, I inhaled sharply through my nose. Obligates around me gasped and shifted their feet. The injury was circular, about the size of a medium coin. The edge was dark with burnt blood, as if Akantha's device had singed the skin. The center was a blistered and bloody oozing mess.

"We have the technology to heal such a wound and leave no scar or trace," Akantha said, her tone almost nonchalant. "But you will wear this wound as a reminder, for the whole lot of you, that there are consequences for disobedience."

I winced, trying to imagine how the girl could keep from screaming in pain. Her arm needed to be dressed or it would get infected. The poor girl needed painkillers right away.

"Line up," Akantha said, flicking her fingers at us with a bored look as if nothing out of the ordinary had happened.

The injured Obligate hadn't yet retrieved her jar of soil— she'd probably been too busy trying to talk to the boy—so I went to the cabinet and got it. I clenched my jaw, trying to hold a neutral expression and avoid looking at Akantha, hoping I wasn't somehow overstepping the rules by carrying the girl's jar.

I let out a small relieved breath only when the Calistan woman began leading us back the way we'd come. I walked in front of the injured girl, a jar in each of my hands, listening to her ragged breaths and whimpers.

Instead of going back outside, we walked through white hallways. At some point we took a turn and passed through a glass walkway into another building, and then we were filing through windowless passages of a different sort. Calistans pushing carts of linens, food, clothing, and other items moved back and forth, in and out of swinging doors. I caught brief glimpses of what looked like storage and supply rooms and caught a whiff of freshness and soap that reminded me of washing day.

By the change in the architecture, I guessed we'd left the hospital or processing building where we'd received our implants. The new building was constructed of a dark material that I couldn't identify—something between metal and smooth stone.

It took me several minutes to realize that these Calistans with the carts and supplies were probably servants. As when we were outside, each one bowed to Akantha. And they all eyed the jars of soil and examined me and the other Obligates as if we were well-fed pigs going up for auction at market.

We went up many flights of stairs—I stopped counting after fourteen—and Akantha let us into a large, half-circle room, with tiered seating lining the curved wall.

"This is where Lord Toric will receive you later tonight," Akantha said. She gestured to a raised platform along the flat wall, where there was a large carved wooden chair.

Memories of the pavilion back home came to mind. There was hardly time to look around before Akantha herded us through a little arched alcove to one side of what I assumed was Lord Toric's throne. I crowded in with the other Obligates and looked down a narrow hallway lined with doors on both sides.

"Males, one to each room over here." Akantha gestured to our right. "Females, this side." She gestured to the doors on the left.

Again, I felt a bit like livestock. I handed the wounded girl her jar, which she took with a tight nod. Her face was pale and constricted with pain. My heart went out to her, but there was nothing more I could do.

I went to the third door on the left, drew a deep breath, and reached for the handle. The door swung open smoothly, revealing a small room that looked . . . comfortable, actually. I whipped around when the door snapped closed behind me, and there was another quick click of a lock sliding into place. I reached for the handle, but as I'd expected the door didn't budge.

I sighed, suddenly bone-weary. If I had to be trapped here, I might as well rest a moment. The heightened sensations I'd felt when I first woke with the implant were fading along with my energy, and I almost wondered if I'd imagined them.

There was a backless divan against the far wall of a space that was larger than the room I'd shared with Lana. Next to it stood a small table with a dark stone pitcher and clear drinking glass. And food.

As I looked around for a spot to set my jar, my stomach rumbled. I'd barely eaten anything in the past two days. A tiny ledge that jutted from the wall next to the door had an indentation that perfectly accepted the base of the jar.

I went to the cart, filled the glass, and drank until it was empty. The dry air made me feel brittle, as if I could never get enough water. I filled the glass again and sipped from it as I bent over the tray of food.

A small oblong loaf of brown bread, a tiny round dish with dark vinegar in it by the aroma, a few thin slices of cured meat, and—

I covered my mouth with one hand, stifling a tiny laugh even as tears sprang to my eyes. There were two bergamines on the tray.

Was it possible that these fruits had come from the very orchard where I'd worked so many days? Could these be bergamines from my very own collection bag, perhaps picked the last day that Court and I had . . . I squeezed my eyelids closed and shook my head. Court did not deserve to take up any space in my mind.

But thoughts of home seemed to sap my strength further, and I sank to the divan. I absently ran my fingers over its fabric. It was nicer than anything from home, nicer than anything I'd ever seen, in fact. The little table was beautifully constructed as well. It shouldn't surprise me—of course the overlords had fancy things. But I was a slave, regardless of how I fared in the competition against the other Obligates. It seemed odd that a room for a slave to rest in should have such lovely things.

I reached for the bread and ate slowly, hoping my stomach wouldn't rebel after so many hours without food.

I touched the implant and traced the edge of the metal disc where it met my skin. The skin there was sensitive, but not painful. I could still feel the faint pulse of the device.

There was a soft click at the door, and it swung inward. I

rose to my feet, my heart lurching.

A woman—an Earthen woman—stepped into the room. She wore a tunic and loose trousers made of a lovely emerald green fabric. Her brown hair was streaked with white. She seemed nearly old enough to be my grandmother, yet she moved with a grace and sensuality that gave her a youthful energy.

"Maya, I am Iris," she said, stopping a few feet away and folding her hands at her waist. "It is my job to offer you guidance during the competition."

A hot bolt of emotion shot up through my chest. This woman was a friend, I knew it immediately, and it was so unexpected I nearly wept.

I went to her and held out my hand. "I'm very pleased to meet you, Iris," I said, my voice wobbling. "I didn't know I would have a personal guide."

"I have been where you now stand," she said, squeezing my hand and then letting it go. "I'll do my best to help you prepare for each phase of the competition."

"You were—?" My eyes widened. "Oh! You won when you were an Obligate? And you're part of Lord Toric's harem?"

She shook her head with a faint smile. "Not Lord Toric's. I was a woman of Lord Alec's harem—Lord Toric's father. But I am now retired."

I felt heat rise to my cheeks as I realized my mistake. She'd served the previous Lord, probably before I was even born. "You're allowed to just . . . retire?"

"The women of the harem still have duties even after we're finished serving as companions to the Lord." She sat on the divan and patted the cushion next to her. "But that is a far-off concern. Let us focus instead on more immediate things. Our time is limited, and I imagine you have many questions."

I sat and angled my knees toward her, relishing the chance to speak to someone who seemed concerned about my welfare. "Yes, I do. I hardly know where to begin." I blinked several times, and then suddenly remembered Akantha's punishment of one of the female Obligates. "There was an Obligate who was injured—burned. Her wound looked extremely painful and needs to be dressed. Is there some way to make sure she gets help?"

Iris inclined her head and reached out a soothing hand to touch my forearm. "Do not worry over her. She will receive the care that the Mistress of Tournament judges she is allowed." She shifted, crossed one leg over the other, and clasped her hands around her knee. "You need to turn your attention to yourself and your own survival, Maya."

My mouth went dry at her grave tone. "Yes, of course. I suppose I want to know, well, what will I face in the first round of the competition?"

"The first challenge of the Tournament of the Offered will be a test of physical and mental fortitude. It is to cull the weak."

Cull the weak? I shivered at the ominous phrase.

"But won't the men have a huge advantage in that type of contest, if it depends on physical strength?" I asked.

"It is not a straight contest of strength," she said. "I don't know the specific nature of this challenge, as the guides aren't informed of the exact details, but it will be something in which a strong young woman will have just as good a chance at surviving as a strong young man."

My chest seemed to contract, squeezing the air out of my lungs. "Some Obligates will die." I barely managed to whisper it.

Part of me felt foolish even saying it. I knew some stages of the competition would be deadly, but knowing such a thing back on Earthenfell and hearing it now on Calisto were somehow two entirely different things.

"Surely you expected this? It is not a secret, even on Earthenfell."

"No, I knew it. It's just—why? Why must the overlords *kill* some of us?" I shook my head in frustration as cold fear gripped me. "Why can't Lord Toric simply look us over and pick his favorite woman for his harem, pick an able man to serve him, and then send the rest back? It just seems extremely cruel and unnecessary."

"There are several reasons," she said. "You must understand that from the Calistans' perspective, it is not about *killing* anyone. It is about sorting the worthy form the unworthy. When the Lord leads the Calistans for the Return to Earthenfell after all enemies have been vanquished, the women of the harem will bear his children, the first children of the new Earth. Those women must be worthy of a responsibility so important and sacred to the Calistans."

My jaw dropped in surprise. This was the first I'd heard of this. As far as I'd known, the harem existed just to serve the pleasure of the Calistan Lord.

"And second, your suggestion is forbidden by the Calistan sacred texts," she continued. "No one from Calisto may set foot on Earthenfell until all others who claim rights to the homeland are defeated."

"What sacred texts? I've never heard of these. And I'm not *from* Calisto. Earthenfell is my home. I was born there and breathed every breath there until today. I've never even read these sacred texts you speak of! Why must I follow their rules?" My fingers dug into the cushion of the divan, every muscle in my body tightening in outrage.

"The Calistans live by their sacred texts, and they handle Earthens according to what the texts direct. Maya, Earthenfell *was* your home, but not anymore." Iris's eyes hardened. "They only possible way you may step foot there again is if the Calistans defeat their enemies within your lifetime and the Lord leads the Return to the homeland."

I sat there, rigid with frustration and fear. "And how long have the Calistans been fighting their enemies?" I whispered.

"Over a thousand years."

I squeezed my eyes closed as anger churned through me in a dark torrent. I wanted to tear through the walls, to scream, to find the so-called sacred texts and shred them and burn the pieces. It was not fair.

It was not fair.

But I could change nothing if I died in the competition. I had to get close to Lord Toric to have any hope of influence.

"I can guess what you are thinking," Iris said.

I opened my eyes and cast her a stony look.

"But you'd best take care to control your feelings because the overlords *know* what you are thinking."

A chill crept up my back and over my scalp, cooling my anger. "What do you mean?"

She reached up to touch the metal disc at the back of my neck. "They will be alerted to any traitorous thoughts. And traitorous actions will bring immediate punishment."

"They can read our thoughts?" My stomach tightened and bile rose in my throat. The idea that my mind was no longer my own was so horrible, so invasive. I clenched my hands together in my lap to keep from clawing at the implant.

"I don't think it works exactly like that, no. Or if they can read our thoughts, I don't think they have any interest in examining every whim that passes through our minds." She gave a short, mirthless laugh. "I imagine that would get very tiresome. But there are certain thoughts they're interested in. Traitorous or murderous ones, for instance. Thoughts that might interfere with the practices outlined in their sacred texts."

I stared at the floor, trying to process the information. Regardless of what my implant did or did not reveal to the overlords, I didn't have time or energy to waste on anger.

Squaring my shoulders, I turned to my guide.

"Okay. So tell me: how do I win?"

She smiled, her eyes crinkling at the outer corners, and patted my knee, clearly relieved to be moving on to a different topic. "I do like your spirit, Maya. You had a physical job on Earthenfell, is that correct?"

"I worked in the orchards picking fruit." I wasn't sure if that qualified as physical work or not. Most work assignments required some moving around.

"Ah yes, I had friends who were fruit collectors. That's good. I can tell that climbing trees has made you lean and strong. You will need to use what you know in order to survive the first challenge. Your body knows how to climb and how to carry heavy collection bags while you balance in precarious places, right?"

"I suppose that's true, and maybe it will be of some use," I said slowly, barely daring to allow a bit of hope lift my heart. "But what advice can you give me?"

"You need to be careful of the other Obligates. Be very careful of who you trust. They're all trying to survive, too, and some will try to manipulate you. Some may even try to kill you."

My eyes widened. "But you said the implants would alert the overlords if we had murderous thoughts."

"During the challenges, they care only if your murderous thoughts are directed toward Calistans. Among the Obligates, almost anything goes. Outright attempts at murdering other

Obligates will figure into the standings of favor, however."

"Standings of favor?"

"You all will be ranked. Boys against each other and girls against each other. Cold-blooded murder, although not literally forbidden, would hurt your standing. Lord Toric would not want a murderous woman in his harem. But being too nice to the other competitors, or being too gullible, will weaken you at best and at worst could kill you."

I snorted a laugh. "So I need to be something less than a cold-blooded killer but more than a doormat."

She smiled faintly, but her eyes were intent. "Yes. Keep in mind that Lord Toric wants not only a woman who can skillfully serve his pleasure in his harem in the near term, but a woman who is worthy of bearing his Earthly children in the event of the Return to the homeland."

I looked at her curiously, wondering about the skills that had won her a place in the harem. "Were you one of the Obligates who was prepared for the competition, or did your clan select you by lottery?"

"I trained for nearly three years," she said. "In return for my sacrifice, my clan mates funded my training with a variety of coaches as well as compensated my family."

That's what my clan had done for Belinda and her family. She'd spent nearly two years in training.

I was afraid to ask the next question, but knew the answer was critical. "And how big an advantage will the trained women have over me?"

"Part of my guidance involves honesty, and I will always be honest with you when I am permitted, Maya. So I will not mince words. Their advantage is significant." She paused, watching my face closely. "They don't have any more information than you do in terms of the exact nature of each phase of challenge in the Tournament, but they've been trained for a wide range of possibilities. You will find that the women who were prepared for this are every bit as strong an agile as you are even though they haven't been doing your type of work. They've been coached in strength and agility, charm, wit, poise, and the arts of seduction and pleasure, among other things."

Seduction and pleasure . . .

I bit my lower lip, considering all of what she'd said. "I'm not . . . experienced." My cheeks heated, and I clutched the fabric of my dress against my palms.

Iris's eyebrows lifted. "You're a virgin?"

I nodded. "I'm um, I—had a boyfriend for a time. So I'm not completely unfamiliar with what goes on between men and women."

She nodded, but peered at me with an assessing gleam in her eye.

"Is that another big mark in the disadvantage column for me?" My entire body seemed to be blushing, but I forced myself to return her steady eye contact.

"Possibly . . . but maybe not." She pressed her lips together for a moment, and then her gaze softened and she leaned in just a bit. "But you know what? That is a worry for another day. For now, I want you to focus only on the challenge ahead of you. You must make it through this phase before we concern ourselves with your sexual inexperience."

A cold sweat sprang to my chest and prickled over the rest of my skin. Yes, the first challenge. If I didn't survive it, all else was irrelevant.

9

Toric

WHEN I'D RETURNED to my chambers after surveying the Offered, my mind swirled with images of the dark angel.

Maya.

Her name was the beat of a drum in my brain, the rhythm of a primal chant.

And she'd opened her eyes. In spite of what the doctor said, I knew that she'd seen me.

Her eyes were the gray-flecked blue of a stormy Calistan sky. I couldn't get the texture of her skin out of my mind. Heavy cream with a dollop of browned butter to warm it from neutral to . . . something I wanted to touch with the tip of my tongue.

Darafina had been waiting when I returned, as I'd requested of Victor. At first, my heart leapt at the sight of her dark waves of hair, as my mind momentarily transposed Maya's face onto

Darafina's. For the briefest of seconds, I'd almost believed that the dark angel had somehow come here, raced ahead so she could wait for me in my bed chamber.

Of course, reality quickly straightened me out. My heart and mind knew the woman in my bed wasn't Maya, but my body did not seem interested in receiving the message.

I extinguished every light in my bed chamber except a single candle on a stand near the door. I stripped off my clothing and went to the woman who spread herself before me wearing only her inviting smile.

"I'm delighted to serve at your favor, my Lord," she purred. And she did look extremely pleased.

When she reached out to stroke me, I caught her wrist and pushed her hand away. Her pleased expression faltered. She recovered with a seductive lowering of her eyelids, but I read a wisp of confusion in her energy.

I closed my eyes, and with Maya's face and vibrant energy in my mind, I coupled with Darafina once . . . twice . . . three times.

After I collapsed on my back, sweating and satiated for the moment, Darafina sat up with glazed eyes.

"My Lord, someone has been urgently knocking at your door for some time," she said. "With your permission, I think it best that I leave you to your duties."

I nodded and waved her away. She quickly slipped on a robe and, walking a bit unsteadily, exited out a side doorway. I hadn't even heard the door, but suddenly aware of the time that had passed, I guessed it was probably Victor, there to get me ready to receive the newly arrived Offered. Even if I was late, it was worth it. I couldn't very well go into the throne room with my arousal pointing the way.

I rose, stepped into undershorts, and went to the main door of my bed chamber.

Victor emanated anxious concern that quickly turned to relief. "My Lord, give me just a moment, and I will have your clothes ready." He gestured toward the dressing room.

That he did not mention bathing first told me I was even later than I'd realized.

In my undershorts, I sat at a mirrored counter to wait for one of my personal medics, a man named Tanning. Darafina had inflicted no wounds on me, but it was protocol for the royal medic to check me before I made a public appearance. Tanning quickly looked over my limbs and torso, and then asked me to stand so he could finish his check. Satisfied, he left without having to activate his healing devices.

I put on immaculately pressed white linen pants and tunic, and then stood on a squat stool in front of a full-length mirror. Victor entered the dressing room and circled me, making small adjustments to the drape of my clothing. He clipped simple iron bands around each of my ankles and wrists. Then he took a cologne sprayer from a small wall cabinet and puffed it at me several times from all sides. It was a distillation of seven sacred plants from Earthenfell made in water from the homeland's seven seas. It was a complex, subtle scent of things newborn and green, old and aged, fresh and floral, an indescribably organic richness that was unlike anything else in the world—on our world, at least.

I ran a hand over my mussed hair, short and spikey but wavy when it was allowed to grow, and then Victor held up a crown of two metal bands—one iron and one copper—twisted together. He placed it on my head and I adjusted it, settling it into place.

I turned to him. "How do I look?"

His brows twitched up in a barely-noticeable shift of his expression. He peered at me, uncertainty flickering in his eyes. "I don't believe you've ever asked me that before, my Lord."

I allowed a grin to widen my mouth. "I don't believe I've ever felt quite the way I feel this evening, Victor."

"Well, you look . . . as a Lord should."

I gave a short laugh, stepped off the stool, and nodded to him. "Let's go, then."

I waited in a room tucked under the throne while the audience entered the throne room and settled themselves.

With me were Calvin and Palovich, dressed in their royal guard uniforms of black trousers tucked into black boots and smart gray jackets that bore the circular Lord's Seal in metallic silver.

Akantha, the Mistress of Tournament, also waited in the room, clad in a stylish and flowing dress made of the same synthetic black material as the guards' pants. It was fitted to show off her thin waist, and its wide bell sleeves fanned out when she moved and draped gracefully when her arms went still at her sides.

She came to stand next to me. When I glanced down, her lips smiled pleasantly, but I didn't like the glint in her eyes. "Did you find the Offered to your liking, my Lord?"

My chest constricted, squeezing some of the air from my lungs, but I managed to keep a bland expression. How did Akantha know I'd already surveyed the Earthens? And what was her game in bringing it up now?

"They are as satisfactory as any other offering of Earthens," I said, my tone even.

"Really?" She feigned mild, polite surprise. "There wasn't even one who captured your interest?"

At that, my heart lurched. She couldn't know. Could she?

"No," I said, then turned my back on her.

No matter what, I had to resist allowing her to bait me. I knew she'd been sharing Jeric's bed for the past many months, and she would report my every word, my every twitch, to my brother. My thoughts flew to Maya. My brother must not discover that I favored one of the Offered. He always found a way to use my weaknesses to torment me.

I went to the back of the room, to a cube-shaped glass cabinet that housed the ancient Earthen clay vessel that came out twice a year when the Offered were received by the Lord. It was one of the handful of sacred objects from Earthenfell that only the High Priestess Lunaria and I were allowed to handle.

Holding the vessel in my hands, feeling its solidity and weight and the natural roughness of its surface, brought me a small measure of calm. The rusty-taupe color was flecked white with dryness and age. The arid atmosphere of Calisto would have degraded it to a pile of dust if not for the climate-controlled cabinet that it was stored in.

When the door to the waiting room opened, I brushed past Akantha and went to the doorway. Flanked by Calvin and Palovich, I walked with slow, ceremonial steps down the dimly lit tunnel toward the brighter light of the throne room.

The side of my neck throbbed faintly as my pulse accelerated. The dark angel—Maya—was out there with the rest of the Offered. I could sense her already.

The hallway opened at the base of the throne platform and everyone rose as I entered. The Priestess, in her opalescent shimmering robes, stood waiting. I paused to hand her the clay vessel, and then turned and strode up the handful of steps to the carved wooden chair at the top of the platform. The seat of the throne was shiny with centuries of use. I waited until Calvin and Palovich had taken their places a step down from the throne on my left and right before sitting. A beat later, the Calistans and Earthens filling the tiers sat down in a rustle of clothing.

Below at the foot of the platform, the Priestess and Akantha stood side-by-side facing me.

A tingling charge passed through my entire body as I

tuned into the energies of the hundreds of people gathered. I'd already picked out Maya's signature and it drew me like the siren song from the ancient Earthen stories, but I forced my eyes to sweep the entire audience. My sister Cassi sat with Mother and Jeric in the center front row. Behind them, relatives both close and distant filled the seats. In the section to the left were Victor and my other Earthen manservants. The ones who currently served me sat in the foremost rows and the retired servants behind. On the right were the women of the harem. As with the manservants, my harem sat nearest to the floor and those who had served my father or who had reached the age of retirement lined the rows behind.

Sytoria was shooting daggers from her eyes at Darafina. But Darafina was beaming at me. Clearly word of Darafina's recent time with me—and the great vigor of our coupling on my part—had reached Sytoria. I felt a twinge of sympathy for Darafina, both for the fact that my enthusiasm in bed did not actually have much to do with her and for the ways that Sytoria would likely punish Darafina for receiving my attention.

I recognized other officials—Council members, high-ranking military men, royal artists and musicians, holy men and women from the Temple of the Mother Earth, and some of Calisto's master craftsmen and women—peppered throughout the top few rows.

I finally allowed myself to shift focus to the Offered, who were standing in a solemn line in the center of the floor, holding their offering vessels and facing me.

As I surveyed the Offered left to right, pausing for a moment on each one, my attention snagged when I got to Maya, fifth from the left. Her chin was lifted, her lips firmed just so, to give her a subtle air of defiance. But underneath, I detected her apprehension.

Her eyes rose to meet mine, and a cacophony of conflicting vibrations seemed to burst around her. I drew a sharp breath in through my nose and pried my gaze from her, shifting to the next Offered. As much as my eyes wanted to remain on her, I could not allow myself to single her out.

When I reached the end of the line, I nodded to the Priestess and Akantha. "You may begin."

They both inclined their heads and then turned to face the Offered.

"Come forward to make your gift and your introduction to Lord Toric," Akantha said, her voice ringing out through the chamber.

Akantha took an almost too-obvious dark pleasure in commanding the young Earthen men and women. Not for the first time, I observed that power over others seemed to fuel her.

The first of the Offered, a strong-looking young man with a calm demeanor, walked forward with his vessel of Earthen soil. He poured the soil into the bowl the Priestess held out and then knelt to set his jar on the floor between Akantha and the Priestess.

Standing with his spine straight and his shoulders pulled

back, he raised his eyes to me. "My Lord, my name is Orion. I humbly give this bit of the homeland in your name and offer myself into your service. I will serve you with honesty, integrity, and loyalty." He inclined his head for a long beat.

I gave a slight nod of acknowledgment, and Orion returned to his place in line. The Offered composed their own introductions, and I immediately liked this young man's introduction as well as the energetic aura he gave off—he appeared unpretentious and even-keeled. He was also well built, and if he'd been born Calistan, he might have made a fine guard.

With effort, I managed to at least remember the names of the next two: Amet and Erin.

The fourth Offered, an attractive young woman with wide eyes and chin-length reddish-brown hair, bore a painful-looking welt on one arm. I shot a glance at Akantha, wondering what offense had prompted her to mark the girl right before the introduction ceremony. Whatever it was, the Mistress of Tournament had clearly not seen fit to repair the damage of the punishment. Akantha knew that it would affect the girl's standing of favor. I stifled a sigh. I would have no choice but to rank her—she introduced herself as Larisa—among the lower of the women at the end of the ceremony. It wasn't just about a physical defect, but what it signified: Larisa was disobedient.

Larisa made her offering and went back to the line. It was Maya's turn.

Now with an excuse to center my full attention on her, I

drank her in.

Her face had paled slightly, maybe due to nerves, making the contrast between her skin and dark hair even lovelier. She shifted the jar in her hands to pour out its contents. Her hands were delicate, her fingers slender, but her movements were sure.

When she lifted her eyes to mine, I had to remind myself to keep breathing.

"I am Maya, my Lord. I bring with me a bit of Earthenfell in my hands and my peoples' prayers for the annihilation of our enemies in my heart. I offer myself into your service with the hope that we will return to Earth in our lifetimes."

There were a few murmurs in the audience at her mention of enemies, and louder murmurs when she made reference to the Return to the homeland. My lips twitched in the start of an appreciative smile before I could compose myself.

It was not the sort of thing the Offered usually said when they introduced themselves, but . . . it stirred something deep within me. I liked that she acknowledged the larger purpose of her presence here, rather than simply trying to ingratiate herself to me. It was an unprecedented introduction that carried an undercurrent of a battle cry.

I couldn't imagine that Maya's personal handler had advised her to say something so bold, but perhaps it was in fact a calculated move. Or maybe in the end her handler had simply lost the argument.

Maya stood there, looking up at me with an impressively

confident set of her shoulders. It took me a moment to realize she was waiting for me to dismiss her. I inclined my head at a slight angle as one corner of my mouth lifted. I couldn't help it—she'd surprised me, and I had to acknowledge it. Was it my imagination, or did her brows twitch up ever so slightly in reply to my slight smile?

My body filled with a warm glow, a surge of life, as I watched her stride back to the line. She'd surprised not only me but nearly everyone in the throne room, if the shifting and low comments that continued to whisper through the space were any indication.

The next Earthen, a shapely young woman with beautiful gold hair and pillowy pink lips, stood waiting for the noise to die down, her confident smile directed right at me. Her expression clearly said that she, at least, wasn't at all impressed by Maya's introduction.

When she walked forward, slowly with her hips swaying and her chest out, I understood why. Just by the way she moved, it was clear she'd had preparation for the Tournament of the Offered.

As she emptied her vessel into the Priestess's bowl, she glanced up at me from under her half-lowered lids, unlike all of the others who had kept their attention on the ceremonial bowl.

Then she knelt almost primly with her knees to the side and her eyes on me while she placed her empty vessel with the others on the floor. When she stepped back, she looked up at me fully and her open, warm yet seductive smile somehow seemed to convey that she knew me, that she'd known me for some time and had guessed things about me that no one else knew.

"My Lord," she said, lowering her lids and inclining her head. When she looked up again, her face was a shade more serious. She continued in an invitingly smooth voice. "My name is Kalindi. It is my greatest honor and deepest pleasure to stand before you today to offer you the essence of Earthenfell." She paused to gesture to the Priestess's bowl of soil with one graceful hand. "And to offer you the essence of myself—my body, mind, and spirit. I have been looking forward to this day for so very long, and my only hope in life is that you find me worthy to serve you."

Kalindi was impressive in every way, and I couldn't deny that her introduction had been perfectly delivered. Even more remarkable was the energy she emanated, which confirmed that her words were sincere—she truly and wholeheartedly wanted to be here and desired to serve me. She was the very embodiment of what any Lord would look for in a woman for his harem.

I dismissed her, and my eyes flicked involuntarily from Kalindi as she turned to rejoin the other Offered to Maya, who stiffened as Kalindi took her place in line and bumped against Maya's arm.

I received the rest of the Offered, memorizing their names and mentally re-ordering their ranks of favor after each one presented. But all the while, part of my attention kept bouncing between Maya and Kalindi, at the contrast between the two of them.

By the time the last young Earthen had poured out his offering, introduced himself, and stepped back into line, my stomach was tight with anticipation. I knew who I wanted to rank first, but I also knew that I would encounter opposition and would make myself vulnerable if I showed my attraction to Maya.

I rose, went down the steps, and turned into the hallway with Akantha and the Priestess following close behind. When the three of us were back in the waiting room—no guards, servants, or other personnel were allowed to be present during the rank of favor deliberations—I turned to the women and drew a deep breath.

Already I could tell this Tournament would not be an easy one. For me or for the Offered.

10

Maya

IRIS HAD PREPARED me for what to expect, and all of us Obligates had emerged from our dressing rooms for a brief walk-through of the introduction ceremony in the empty throne room. But later when we filed into the packed space, my heart pounded in my ears and nerves gripped my stomach.

I managed to register that the center section of the audience was filled with Calistans, while mostly Earthens sat in the sections on either side. It was shocking somehow to see dozens of Earthens gathered here, so very far away from our home. So many sacrifices, men and women over many generations who had left their families and homes never to return.

I tried to scan for familiar faces—I'd known some of the Obligates by name from the past few Selections—before I remembered that most of the Obligates would not have ended up here. The majority of the Obligates who left Earthenfell ended up dead in the competition or sent away to other lands. Only the winners sat in this room—one man and one woman from each Selection. A manservant and a lady of the harem. Thirty-two young men and women came here from Earthenfell each year, and each year twenty-eight of them were losers.

When Lord Toric entered the chamber, my focus narrowed to him and everything else faded to the background. I had a sense of déjà vu, a strange feeling that I knew the details of his face as if I'd seen him in a dream. His stature was large and solid, even for a Calistan man. With his broad shoulders, the squared masculine set of his jaw, and his intense aquamarine eyes, he was a striking figure. Back on Earthenfell, I'd always imagined that the Lord of the overlords would be an imposing, intimidating man. He commanded the space as I'd expected, but Lord Toric in the flesh had more layers and depth than the image I'd had in my mind.

No doubt the real Lord Toric had the capacity for the anger and violence I'd imagined. But the Lord Toric of my imagination was heartless, a one-dimensional looming figure of authority. In contrast, the man on the throne before me kept his face composed, even stone-like at times, but his eyes betrayed his curiosity, boredom, surprise, warmth, amusement, and other subtle emotions and shifts.

The introductions of the Obligates who went before me were a blur. But when Lord Toric's gaze fell on me, everything snapped into such sharp focus it nearly stole the breath from my lungs. I gathered myself as best I could and tried to look and sound confident. I counted it a small victory that my voice didn't shake during my introduction.

Iris and I had debated about my introduction, and she'd advised me to go with something less controversial, but I'd refused. When she realized she wasn't going to sway me, she cautioned me that the nature of my introduction would draw attention and possibly criticism. She'd warned me that some might see my words as insolence, maybe even scandalous, coming from a slave, so I was ready for the reaction of the crowd. But I carried on as if all was well. At least, I hoped it appeared that way.

I didn't have enough presence of mind to really analyze the audience's response. Iris was in the audience and I knew she would tell me later what she thought. She'd strongly urged me to temper my introduction, but by Lord Toric's reaction—a subtle yet unmistakable heightened interest and tiny smile of approval—I felt I'd made the right choice.

At the end of the introductions, my eyes lingered on Lord Toric as he, Akantha, and the Priestess disappeared into the darkness of the tunnel under the throne.

A moment later, the Obligate guides rose from their seats, and Iris took her place beside me. As we left with the others in an orderly double line through the door that led to our dressing rooms, I glanced at Iris's face but couldn't read her expression.

Once we were out of the view of the audience, the woman ahead of Iris clutched at her Obligate charge's arm. "You could not have been better," she said to Kalindi. "Impeccable."

It suddenly struck me that Kalindi's guide seemed rather invested in her Obligate's performance. Scanning the other guide-Obligate pairs, I realized several whispered discussions had begun, and the pairs were hurrying into the privacy of the dressing rooms.

As soon as Iris and I were alone in my room, I turned to her and heaved a sigh, tired now that my adrenaline was draining away. "Well? How did I do?"

She clasped her hands at her waist and peered at me earnestly for a moment. "You made a striking impression on Lord Toric. And on the rest of those gathered."

My eyebrows lifted, and I gave her a pointed look as I waited for her to elaborate. When she didn't, I finally asked, "Good or bad?"

She pulled her bottom lip in between her teeth and tilted her head down for a moment, but not before I saw a spark in her dark eyes. She raised her head and gave me a shrewd, appraising look. "I think you have set yourself up as one to watch in this Tournament. And that is good. Very good. Much better than being meek or forgettable. However, because your introduction was unconventional, you may find that this is not as positively reflected in the initial ranks of favor as we would like."

I went to the divan and sat, happy to be able to rest my

feet. It seemed like I'd been awake for days. It had to be the middle of the night back on Earthenfell. Maybe even early morning. I hadn't been near a window in many hours and had no idea of the time.

"The blonde vixen, Kalindi, is obviously prepared and will score well," Iris continued. "A couple of the other women who were trained will probably score ahead of you, too. But don't worry about that now. We've just gotten started. Now you must ready yourself for a real challenge. One that is much more significant than the introduction."

"Now?" I winced, hoping she didn't actually mean *right* then.

"Yes, now."

I groaned. "I thought we'd have some time, at least be able to sleep . . .?"

Iris shook her head and went to the door. I hadn't noticed the clothing of some sort hanging there. She took the hangers from their hook and brought them to me. "We can keep talking while you change."

I pulled off the black Departure garb, the dress I still thought of as Belinda's. It felt as if I'd been wearing it for days. I hung it on one of the hooks nearby and faced Iris in my underclothes.

"The first challenge begins tonight," she said. She handed me slim, stretchy pants that reminded me of the skin-tight shorts I wore for collecting fruit in the orchards. Like my shorts, these pants were black. The three-quarter sleeved shirt was made of the same fabric, and similarly form-fitting.

I narrowed my eyes at her. "You purposely kept that little detail from me."

"Oh come now, it's not as if I lied to you," she said. She passed me a pair of lightweight black shoes with grippy treaded soles. "But I did it for your own good. I can see that you're the type of woman who needs to take one thing at a time."

I cocked my head as a small smile slipped across my lips. "Lucky guess."

Iris was right. I always did better—whether at school, work, or anything else—when I could focus on completing the task in front of me before worrying about the next thing. Lana was the one who seemed able to juggle many things and hold lots of details in her mind all at once. My nose and eyes prickled with the sudden threat of tears at the thought of my sister.

I ducked my head as I leaned over to pull on the shoes, hiding my face while I tried to compose myself.

When I looked up, Iris tilted her head at the tray of food and water. "You will be glad later if you have something to eat now," she said. "You need to keep your strength up."

The food had been replenished. I wasn't really hungry, but I reached for two thin slices of meat and draped them across a piece of crusty white bread.

Iris sat down on the divan next to me and leaned forward, her face earnest. "Maya, I know you're grieving and exhausted, but you must find a way to light a fire in yourself. You're going to face real danger in this first challenge. Not everyone will come out of it alive."

I chewed for a moment, my mouth suddenly too dry for food. I forced down a swallow and met her gaze, thinking of how the other guides had whispered with their Obligates after the introduction ceremony. "What is your stake in this?"

She pulled her head back a little in surprise. "Stake?"

"Why do you care if I do well? As our advisors, do you and the other guides stand to gain or lose something?" I asked, trying to be as direct as I could.

"I can't discuss that."

I was beginning to wonder how much I could trust her. She seemed to be purposely doling out details of the contest— the Tournament of the Offered, the Calistans called it—in very small tidbits. And now, she was withholding something significant, something that possibly affected the way she prepared me for the challenges. And just as important, it was something that affected how the other Obligates were being coached by their guides, too.

I gave her an unrelenting stare. "You promised me honesty, Iris."

"I promised honesty in all matters that I could discuss with you," she said, returning my hard look. "This is one that I am forbidden to talk about. Even if I wanted to, I couldn't." She pointed at a spot behind her ear, indicating her implant.

"And that goes for the other Obligates, too? Their guides are also withholding this information from them?"

"Yes. Upon my family's name, that is the truth."

She'd said she couldn't discuss it, but hadn't denied that she did have some stake in my performance. Even though I didn't know the details, I could only hope that this was good for me, that it meant she would do what she could to help me perform well. I tried to take some comfort in that thought instead of letting my mind wander to other possibilities . . . such as wagers placed on our performances and that our guides might have a vested interest some of us doing better than others. Such a sobering thought. What if the guides were part of their own game, their own competition? Unless Iris slipped and revealed something she wasn't supposed to—and her implant probably made that impossible—there was no way for me to know. I reached for a purple-red turnibeet and bit into its crisp flesh.

Iris shifted on the divan, crossing her legs and hooking her clasped hands over her knees. "Is there anyone among the Obligates that you know well enough to trust with your life?"

I stopped chewing for a second, taken aback at the abruptness of the question. "No, I don't know any of them that intimately. Recently I've spoken to Orion a handful of times, and I think—" I paused, considering what to say about Orion. I barely knew him and most of my familiarity with him stemmed from our common plight as Obligates. Still, I couldn't help but feel that he was an honorable man and someone I could trust. "Well, I do not know him with the familiarity that comes from many years' friendship, but from our recent interactions, I believe he has a compassionate and trustworthy nature."

"And does Orion know any of the others well? Any of the women, in particular?"

"I don't know. It doesn't seem so. Why would that matter?"

"If he is closer with someone else, he may prefer that person over you."

My brow wrinkled. I wasn't sure what she was getting at.

"If there is an Obligate you believe you can trust, forming an alliance could help you," she said. "By far your safest bet is aligning yourself with a male Obligate because—"

"He and I aren't in direct competition," I finished her sentence for her. "So that's why some of the women were trying to talk to some of the men after we got our implants. The girl who got punished, the one with the bobbed hair, she was trying to talk to Orion when Akantha caught her."

"Did he seem to be entertaining her request?"

"I don't think so, but they didn't really have time to talk about it. We haven't been allowed to speak to each other so far. I assume that restriction will be lifted during this first challenge?" I was trying to imagine what it might be—the challenge to cull the weak—but with no knowledge of the nature of challenges that past Obligated had faced, I couldn't fathom what the overlords had in store for us.

"Yes, you'll get permission to communicate freely."

"Iris, can you tell me about past challenges? The culling one during your tournament as an Obligate, perhaps?"

She blinked, and her eyes grew distant. "Why yes, I can

tell you that," she said after a long pause. "We were dropped on the edge of a rocky cliff overlooking the sea. We were forced to climb down and cling to tiny ledges on the side of the cliff overnight. A storm came in, and the water raged against the rocks below . . ." She trailed off, and her dark eyes shifted around the room but didn't seem to register our surroundings.

"Some of the Obligates . . . fell?"

"Yes. There were fewer ledges than Obligates, so there were tussles between some of the competitors."

The blood seemed to drain from my face. I shivered and curled my arms around my middle. "How did you manage to survive?"

"I went low on the cliff, down to the lowest ledge. I think the others didn't want to come down after me and challenge for my space, especially when the water began to rise. It was a lucky strategy, except that I was—" She stopped and cleared her throat. "I was in an unfortunate position to see the ones who didn't make it. I tried to save one girl who fell, but the tide swept her away, tore her hand right out of mine."

I shivered again as I imagined watching Obligates fall to their deaths, listening to their screams, watching them drown. Drawing a sharp breath in, I gave my head a small shake. That was in the past, and I had to focus on my own battles.

"So I should try to form a partnership with Orion. What else?"

"Beware of the others. The trained ones, especially, may be ruthless."

I clenched my jaw and silently reprimanded myself. I should have paid closer attention to the other Obligates' introductions, instead of ogling Lord Toric. "Besides Kalindi, which of the others seemed trained?"

"Larisa, the one Akantha punished. Meribel, the little waif with the big round eyes, and Britta, the tall athletic-looking one."

I knew who Larisa was of course, and I remembered Meribel and Britta. Neither had the grace of Kalindi, though Meribel possessed an endearing pixie quality. In a physical contest, Britta definitely had an edge. She was tall, slim, and toned, and I recalled that when we were children she enjoyed challenging the fastest boys to footraces and was known for beating most of them.

A chime sounded, and I jumped.

Iris stood. "It's time to return to the throne room. Then you'll be set loose for the challenge." She gripped my shoulders and looked straight into my eyes. "You are strong and intelligent. Keep your head about you, and you will beat this challenge, Maya."

I nodded, suddenly too nervous to speak. She pulled at the end of her braid and then held out something. It was her hair tie. "Pull your hair up, secure it into a knot. One less thing to get in your way or for the others to grab at."

"Thank you." I took the hair tie and did as she suggested.

Outside my dressing room, the others were lining up in Obligate-guide pairs. A welling of gratitude swept through me. I turned to Iris. "Thank you," I whispered. "For being my guide. I do not know whether you had a choice in the matter, but I appreciate that I have you."

She squeezed my forearm. "You are welcome."

Then we were parading back into the throne room. As before, our guides left us to go to their seats in the audience and we Obligates stood shoulder-to-shoulder in the center of the floor, facing the throne.

Lord Toric emerged from the hallway below the throne, flanked by Akantha and the woman in shimmering robes, the High Priestess. The two women stopped at the base of the throne platform, as they had before. Our empty jars had been cleared from the floor.

Once Lord Toric was settled on his carved wooden chair, everyone in the audience sat down with a soft swish of clothing and shuffle of shoes.

Akantha stepped forward. "On behalf of Lord Toric, I present the initial ranks of favor in the Tournament of the Offered." I could have sworn I caught a brief flash of annoyance pass over her face when she said Lord Toric's name. She turned to gesture up at the throne with one slim arm.

I peered up at Lord Toric for a moment before I realized that everyone was looking at the wall above him.

A light in the ceiling shone on the wall, illuminating what appeared to be large tiles stacked on top of each other in two columns. The tiles were blank. Then they all blinked, and images appeared on them. I sucked in a quick breath. Each tile had the likeness of an Obligate's face, with his or her name underneath.

It took me a moment to understand what I was seeing. I found my own tile in the column on the right, the fourth down from the top. Kalindi's face was at the head of the column. Next was Meribel, and then a girl named Cheytan. Britta was immediately after me, in fifth place. Sixth was Larisa, the unfortunate one who had been caught talking to Orion earlier. Four more female faces followed Larisa's tile.

I was fourth out of ten female Obligates. That seemed good, but was it? I wanted to twist around and search for Iris in the crowd, to seek her reassurance, but I resisted. Murmurs of conversation swept through the audience.

Yes, it had to be good. I was ranked ahead of two of the women who had been trained for this competition—Britta and Larisa. Surely that was at least a small achievement?

I glanced over at the men's rankings. Orion was really the only one I knew at all, and he was ranked second. I found I felt just as pleased for him as I did for myself.

When I finally dropped my eyes to the throne, my heartbeat seemed to pause for a moment. The alien Lord was leveling his penetrating gaze right at me. One corner of his mouth stretched in the barest hint of a half-smile, and then his attention flicked elsewhere.

I forced myself to take a breath, dizzy with the sudden conviction that Lord Toric had been trying to communicate something to me. There was no time to ponder it further.

Akantha was speaking again.

"Fifteen minutes from now, the first challenge of this Tournament of the Offered will commence." She smiled and raised her arms to the crowd as if announcing that everyone in the audience was getting a free week's worth of food. Her gaze skipped across us. "The Offered will follow me to be transported to the challenge site."

My stomach knotted and my heart punched against my chest. Would it be something like Iris's challenge? Or worse?

Akantha brusquely walked forward and cut through the middle of our line, and we all turned to trail after her. My eyes sought Iris in the crowd, and I located her sitting toward the back of the harem section. She gave me a firm nod and an encouraging smile.

I took a deep breath and remembered I needed to look for Orion. We hadn't been given permission to speak to each other yet, but I slowed and let a few Obligates pass me until he caught up to me. I glanced up at him; he winked and quirked a tight smile at me. His gaze lingered, and I wondered if his guide had advised him to team up with another Obligate, too.

I'd expected to have to walk for a bit and eventually board some sort of vehicle that would take us to the site of the contest. When the Obligates ahead of me turned into a small room not far from the throne room, I nearly stumbled as my shoes scuffed to a halt.

In front of us was the dizzying, blinding swirl of an open portal.

Akantha stood to one side and swept her icy gaze over us. "This is the way to your first challenge. To conquer it, you simply must survive the night. As soon as you pass through the portal, you are free to speak to each other. Let the challenge begin."

11

Maya

A STIFF, COOL breeze hit my skin before my eyes fully recovered from the bright light of the portal. I took in strange smells and the touch of crisp air on my face. Blinking spots from my vision, I immediately noticed the low angle of the sun—it seemed to be evening wherever we were. I had no idea if we were still on Calisto or had passed through the portal to some other world.

There were a few spindly trees nearby. Old wood creaked under my feet, and I looked down to see that we stood on a platform that was fifteen or twenty feet from the ground. Strange calls of birds and other animals sounded all around us.

I whirled, looking for Orion. Finding him behind me, I clutched at his arm. "Will you team with me? Our odds might be better if we work tog—"

My hasty plea ended in a shriek as the platform under us snapped loudly and then tilted. My arms flailed as I reflexively struggled for balance and screamed again. Just before I pitched over the edge, a strong hand clamped around my upper arm and pulled me to safety.

I looked up into Orion's blanched face. He had a hold on one of the support posts of the platform with one hand, and gripped me with the other.

"We need to get off this thing; it's going to collapse any second," he said.

I nodded breathlessly, vaguely registering his use of "we" and hoping it meant he'd accepted my proposition.

A terrified scream and plea for help came from the other end of the platform. The dry, splintering platform had broken away from one of the four uprights, but a scrap of a plank still hung on the post. An Obligate balanced on it, her arms wrapped around the post.

"Pull me over, please!" the girl was begging the nearest Obligates—Cheytan and Britta.

Britta started to reach across the gap to extend a hand to the girl, but Cheytan swatted her hand away. "Leave her! We can't take any more weight on this side."

Cheytan was probably right—many Obligates were on their hands and knees clinging to the floor planks to keep from sliding off as the platform creaked and sagged. Still, her heartless tone chilled me.

The other Obligates were talking over each other,

wondering where we were, why there wasn't a ladder down. A couple were whimpering or staring silently with wide, shocked eyes.

"Can you make it over to that branch?" Orion asked in my ear.

I followed his gaze to a tall, thin tree, and nodded. We shifted around so I was nearest the tree. I stood on the edge of the plank, balancing with Orion's hand to steady me. The branch I was aiming for required a three-foot jump, which I knew I could make. My bigger concern was whether it would hold my weight.

The platform shifted again, the broken side dropping another couple of feet, and everyone shrieked. I grabbed the support post to keep from toppling backward, found my balance, and jumped.

My stomach hit the branch, my arms wrapping over it. The branch bent and bobbed under my weight, but it held. I quickly swung my feet up and shimmied toward the trunk.

Before I could move to the other side to leave the branch free for Orion, the platform cracked loudly. I turned to see Orion jump just as the plank below him gave way and the entire platform went crashing to the ground. He caught the branch with one hand but then slipped. I gasped as he fell, but he managed to grab the next branch down.

The tree pulled to one side under our weight, its trunk much more flexible than I'd expected. I scrambled around to try to balance out our weight.

Below, there was a cacophony of moans and screams. The Obligates who hadn't already slipped off the platform had plunged to the ground when it fell, and the distance was far enough to break bones.

I squinted in the fading light. Through the trees a sliver of sun balanced on the horizon. Soon it would be dark. I looked around, trying to get a sense of the land. I caught a glimpse of a copse of trees about a third of a mile away that looked taller and much more sturdy than the ones that surrounded us.

I turned to Orion, who'd moved against the trunk. Our tree was still bobbing back and forth from the impact of his weight.

Before I could point out the trees in the distance, several fast-moving dark, bulky forms on the ground drew my attention.

Orion saw them, too. "What are those things?"

A giant hand seemed to squeeze my chest as I watched the creatures streak our way, straight toward the Obligates below.

I sucked in a lungful of air. "Run!" I screamed at them with everything I could muster. "Something's coming! *Run*! Get off the ground!"

At least a few of them seemed to hear me. Some sprinted to nearby trees. Others moved much more slowly due to an array of serious injuries. One of the young men began climbing up one of the still-standing platform supports. A women lay on the ground with her arm twisted behind her at an angle that made my stomach lurch. It was Larisa. It looked like she hadn't moved since she'd fallen.

The dark creatures came barreling in, and I watched in frozen horror. Two of the creatures went after Larisa. A couple of others chased Obligates who were still trying to get to safety. When I saw a flash of jagged teeth and a spray of dark liquid, I turned away and squeezed my eyes closed, praying that Larisa was already dead. My entire body began to tremble as the warm metallic smell of blood hit my nose.

"Maya." Orion's fingers dug into my shoulder. "We need to get away from here."

I kept my eyes closed and shook my head violently. "We can't go down there."

"We can't stay," he said, his voice low and urgent. "Look."

I opened my eyes and looked to where he was pointing. One of the creatures—it appeared to be something between a dog and a bear—had its front paws high up on the post where a boy was perched. The creature sniffed the air and then emitted a rumbling growl. It dropped back to the ground, but instead of slinking away, it gathered itself and then sprang into the air with surprising power.

It jumped high enough to nip at the boy's foot, and he cried out and pulled himself another couple of feet up the post.

A new terror ripped through me. We weren't high enough. I scrambled up a few branches with shaking, sweaty hands, but the tree's trunk was too thin. It began to list to one side and then bend.

My mind raced as I clung to the trunk and swiveled my

head around, looking for any escape, any greater safety.

"Orion, one of us has to get off this tree," I said in a panicked whisper, not wanting to draw the attention of the snarling, snapping creatures. I pointed. "If we bend the trunk that way, I can jump to the next one. Then we can both climb a little higher."

He nodded and came around to my side, and I crawled out onto a branch. We both threw our weight to my side, trying to bend the tree toward its neighbor. I leapt. Leaves and small branches whipped at my face and forearms, but I managed to hold on.

I turned to make sure Orion was still secure where he was. His gaze was cast down. Two of the creatures prowled around Orion's tree, muscles rippling under their fur. Then one of them reared back and sprang. It didn't hit anywhere near Orion, but the impact caused the trunk to jerk and swing violently.

Orion threw me a wild-eyed look as he hugged the trunk with his arms and legs. The two creatures prowled again, now circling my tree, too.

A strangled terrified scream ripped through the forest. Both of the creatures turned, half-rising on their hind legs, and then sped away toward the noise.

"Orion, there's a better spot not far from here," I hissed urgently.

I was already dropping down through the branches, my heart in my throat. I let go and flew down the last several feet, landing with a thud. I took off as fast as I could, heading in the direction of the copse of thick, sturdy trees I'd seen earlier.

When I heard pounding feet behind me, I turned only long enough to make sure it wasn't the creature's. Orion was a couple of yards back, and the boy who'd been on the post trailed behind him. I thought I caught a glimpse of one of the female Obligates following, too.

Sucking air into my lungs and pumping my elbows hard, I flew across the soft mat of dirt and decaying leaves. In a corner of my mind, I wondered if we were back on Earthenfell, if we'd passed through the portal only to be deposited in some strange corner of the Ten Protected Zones or maybe completely outside the shield.

But our location wasn't important. All that mattered was staying alive.

Someone came up beside me, and I let out a strangled shriek of surprise and nearly stumbled to the ground. It was Britta, striding with an almost easy-looking gait.

"Where?" she panted, glancing at me.

I hesitated, remembering Iris's warning. Would Britta betray me somehow? I decided to chance it. I pointed. "Those trees. We'll be safer up there."

When we reached the copse, I went right to the thickest tree, hoping Britta wasn't going to try to challenge me for it. To my relief, she chose a different tree. Just as I pulled myself up to the first branch and swung my feet off the ground, Orion and the other boy raced up and began climbing trees, too.

Fragrant sap stuck to my hands, and I noticed these trees had bark similar to the conifers back home, but instead of needles they had long fronds that grew in bunches, like little hand brooms. I sent out a silent prayer that the sap wasn't some sort of toxin like that of the poison vines back home. The last thing I needed was an inflamed, oozing rash.

When I got high enough to begin to feel some measure of safety, I paused to catch my breath and wipe my sweaty brow with my arm. The sun was down, but there was a bit of faint light left in the sky.

I began pulling at branches, bending them toward each other, twisting a few of them around and through each other to form a sort of loosely-woven seat. Not as sturdy as the nest Court and I had made in the orchard, but enough to cradle me so I could curl up and let my exhausted, shaking muscles rest.

I was tempted to call out to Orion but was too afraid of drawing the attention of the dog-bear creatures or any other predators that might be nearby.

I reached out, feeling for a small branch with enough heft that it might be used as a weapon but small enough that I could break it off. When I found one that seemed suitable, I held my breath and pulled at it. The crack as it snapped seemed to report out through the quiet forest like a gun shot. I froze, listening. The birds had silenced at some point, and I wasn't sure what was more eerie—the quiet or the unfamiliar chirps and calls of before.

I stripped the leaves and smaller twigs from the stick,

deciding that we definitely weren't on Earthenfell. The creatures that hunted us, that had fallen upon Larisa and killed at least one other Obligate as I'd sped away, were not Earthen.

Clutching the stick, I felt the jagged end where it had broken off and imagined how I'd jab it into a creature's eye or snout. But I was fairly certain the dog-bears couldn't reach me. Their muscular bodies and sharp claws might allow them to jump to a low branch, but they didn't seem agile enough to be true climbers.

As the hours passed, my adrenaline faded and weariness seeped deep into my bones. How long had it been since I'd slept? It had been late evening on Earthenfell when we'd passed through the portal to Calisto. Was it morning yet back home? Were Mother and Lana making coffee? Maybe Lana was already in the orchard, back at work after the weekend.

I pressed my fingers to my mouth as I imagined Lana going to work without me. Who was guiding her? I hadn't thought of that part, only of making sure her quota was met. My chest tightened at the thought of someone else taking her elbow, walking her to the orchard and settling her under a tree with her canteen and skeins of dyed thread.

Sadness pulled at me and a heavy ache settled in my stomach. This was the first time I'd ever been away from home. I'd never imagined it was possible to feel this homesick. I'd never imagined I'd have *reason* to feel this homesick. But I was too exhausted even to cry.

I tipped my head back, trying to blank my mind, and

watched as night darkened the forest. After some time, a spectacular swath of stars lit the sky enough to throw faint shadows. The beauty was comforting at first, until it struck me that I did not know these stars. They were arranged in unfamiliar patterns with none of the constellations I'd been taught to pick out as a child.

It made me feel even farther away from everything and everyone I loved. I pulled my legs to my chest, closed my eyes, and rested my forehead on my knees. I kept dozing and then waking with a start, my heart pounding.

When something rustled my hair, I mumbled, swatting at whatever was trying to interrupt my dream of sunshine and bergamine trees.

A sharp stab at my shoulder brought me fully awake, my heart thumping with alarm. Faint reddish-orange light was brightening the sky. I had no idea how long I'd been asleep. Or how long the night lasted there, for that matter.

Disoriented, I swiveled around trying to see what had jabbed at me. There was a rustle of movement to my left, and I whipped that way, brandishing my stick.

I saw nothing, and for a moment wondered if I'd been hallucinating.

A soft warbling drew my attention upward. A huge black eye peered down at me, and I let out a strangled scream and tried to scramble back. Just a few feet away sat the largest bird I'd ever seen. Its beak was as long as my arm, gracefully curving down to a point. Its wickedly serrated talons gripped its perch.

I flailed for a breathtaking second, nearly losing my balance before my fingers found a handhold.

The bird hopped down a branch, coming closer, and I froze. It peered at me with one eye, seeming to size me up, and then dipped its head toward me. I gasped and jerked back. I couldn't take my eyes off the sharp point of its beak. One peck would probably crack my skull open like an egg.

Keeping my eyes on the bird, I blindly reached for another branch, aiming to creep out of the bird's reach and hoping it would lose interest in me. I dropped my feet to a branch below and slowly lowered myself.

The bird hopped down a level, still peering at me with avian curiosity. A string of curses streamed through my mind.

Suddenly its head darted forward, the beak snapping. I jerked back, but not fast enough. The sharp sting at my shoulder shocked me into dropping my stick. It knocked through the branches below and landed on the ground.

The bird cawed and opened its long beak, and started to fan out its wings. I flipped over onto my stomach, kicked my feet around until I found a foothold below, and started dropping down through the branches as fast as I could go.

Flapping and rustling sounds above told me the bird was in pursuit. I screamed as it swished down with a flap of wings and raked at my arm with its claws.

In my panic I lost my handholds, and for a moment I was flying. I landed with a hard thud on my left side, bruising my hip and jamming my shoulder. Scrambling, I frantically searched for my stick. There! I grabbed it and spun, swinging out blindly.

The bird had followed me to the ground, and it wasn't alone. Another one danced near me on light feet, its enormous wings spread. I swiped, and it hopped back out of my reach.

Then two more birds alighted from the trees. They were calling to each other, surrounding me in a shrinking half-circle of terrifying feathered creatures that stood as tall as me.

My heart in my throat, I edged backward toward the nearest tree, hoping to use the trunk to shield myself from the back.

One bird hopped and flapped its wings, darting straight for me. I fell to the ground and covered my head, shrieking as white-hot pain exploded across my upper back. It came again, raking my shoulders and back with its claws, this time actually clutching me long enough to drag me forward several feet.

It wanted to carry me away, and I suddenly realized it was strong enough to do so.

I heard a voice, curses and hollering, but I was afraid if I looked up I'd get clawed across the face.

When the bird let me go, I finally dropped my arms to look. Orion, Britta, and the other boy were yelling at the birds and throwing rocks.

It seemed to be working. The birds were cawing and dancing around but had stopped their attack.

I ran in a crouch to the other Obligates, scooping up my stick and a couple of fist-sized rocks as I went.

The sun was nearly up now. My mouth went dry as I caught a clear glimpse of something through the trees. A dark shape, prowling my way.

"Orion, it's one of those things, those creatures," I said urgently over the noise of cawing and the Obligates' hollering.

The birds had noticed, too. One took off with great whooshes of air as it flew away. A couple more flapped up to perch on low nearby branches, as if settling themselves to watch how we'd deal with this new threat.

I eyed the dog-bear. It was circling wide around us and sniffing the air.

"What do we do?" I whispered, my voice shaking.

"Three more, over there," Britta said.

I heard the low growls before I saw the creatures.

Terror spiked through me. We couldn't take refuge in the trees. We couldn't outrun the giant dog-bears.

They circled closer now, baring their teeth at us. One of them lunged—not an attack, but just a test. I hollered and jabbed my stick at it, and it retreated.

There was a brightening point of light in my peripheral vision, but I didn't dare take my eyes off the creatures.

Another creature lunged and snapped, and again I stabbed out with my stick.

"The portal!" Orion said.

I risked a look. He was right, a portal was forming a few yards away.

"We need to hurry," I said. "We don't know how long

they'll leave it open."

As a group, we began taking cautious steps toward the light. This seemed to agitate the creatures. One lunged and caught Britta by the ankle, and she went down hard on her side as it jerked her foot out from under her.

I lunged forward and jabbed, aiming for the creature's face. I struck it in the snout and it whimpered and let go of Britta. Orion hauled her up by one arm and dragged her along with him.

We were almost there.

"The portal is blinking, we need to go!" hissed the boy whose name I still didn't know.

"On three," I said. "One, two, three!"

I turned and raced toward the light. The sounds of snarling and pounding feet drove me forward.

I leapt, throwing myself at the portal. Just as I passed through, I heard an agonizing scream.

I whipped around, trying to see who it was, but the blinding light of the portal obscured whatever was happening on the other side. Orion burst through, half-dragging and half-carrying Britta.

I stared at the portal, holding up one hand to shield my eyes. Seconds ticked by. Finally I turned to Orion, who had fallen to one knee, panting hard.

He looked up at me and shook his head. "The creatures got him."

"Did you even know his name?" I whispered.

"His name was Anders." Orion closed his eyes.

"You survived the first phase."

I turned at the sound of a new voice. It was Akantha.

There were two more portals nearby, and a handful of other Obligates who looked as haggard as Orion, Britta, and me. Everyone had scratches or bleeding wounds. Some favored limbs, groaning in agony.

The portals contracted and then winked out. I did a quick count. Five men and seven women. Four Obligates had not returned.

"You will have your injuries repaired, and then you will go to your quarters to bathe and sleep," Akantha said.

A hot wave of anger swelled up through me at her nonchalant tone. I stood, my arms tensed and my fingers clenched into trembling fists. "And how soon will you inform the families of the dead?"

She turned on me and pulled herself up to her full height, her glowering face looming over me. "That is not your concern, girl."

I stared up at her, knowing that if I responded she'd bring out the wand she'd used to burn Larisa's arm, but unable to back away. I bit down hard on the insides of my cheeks, struggling to keep in check the tirade that I wanted to hurl at her.

"Something else you want to say?" she asked with a smirk.

I finally lowered my gaze and shook my head.

"Line up," she commanded. "The medics are waiting for you in the next room."

I obediently followed Akantha along with the rest of the Obligates, but inside fury was burning me up. Iris had convinced me that the Calistans believed it was necessary to cull the unworthy Obligates—the ones who were weak. I found it abhorrent, but I understood that the Calistans believed in the practice as it was dictated by their sacred texts.

But had Anders been unworthy? Larisa, who'd fallen off the platform and been devoured by the creatures? To me, it simply appeared to be bad luck, not unworthiness or weakness. And for all I knew, the other two Obligates who died in the forest had been similarly unlucky.

It just as easily could have been me who fell off that platform or who was caught by the dog-bears as we raced to the portal. I could have been one of the unlucky ones.

It terrified me, but it also made me furious. How could the Calistans play with others' lives this way? How could they *live* with themselves?

And what could I do about it?

This question pounded through my aching head as I sat on a hospital bed in my underclothes. A medic smeared a cool gooey substance over the deep, burning cuts on my back and shoulders, and the pain immediately began to fade. She worked on my shoulder, where the bird's sharp beak had ripped deeply into my flesh, for several minutes with a handheld device. It was excruciating when the device first contacted the wound, but I steeled myself, sitting there like a stone and staring straight ahead. Finally she put the device aside and smeared gel on my shoulder.

After all my injuries had been attended to, she pointed at a pile of fabric and then left. I lifted it and discovered it was a simple cotton tunic dress. Seeing no clean underclothes, I left on the ones I wore and slipped the dress over my head, and then sat on my bed.

"Line up," Akantha called several minutes later.

I stepped beyond the curtains that separated my bed from those on either side and watched as the rest of the Obligates did the same. The women wore tunics like mine, and the men wore only loose-fitting drawstring pants made of the same material.

Akantha took us through windowless corridors that felt as if they were near the bottom of the palace, maybe even underground.

I wrapped my arms around my waist as I began to wonder if we'd be locked up in cells, in some dungeon deep in the bowels of the palace.

In a quiet hallway, Akantha stopped and turned to us. "The doors are marked with your names. Use the next several hours to bathe and sleep."

I glanced at the nearest door. It had a tile with Britta's face on it and her name printed underneath, just like the tiles on the wall that had shown our ranks of favor. I wondered bitterly if someone had come down ahead of us to remove the names of the dead from their doors.

I found mine, and when I opened the door, I paused in

surprise. The room was small, but luxurious by standards back home. There was a bed made up with crisp-looking sheets, a table with a lamp, and a simple chair. Through a doorway to the right, I spotted the rim of a soaking tub.

The medic had healed my wounds and aches, but there was no cure for the exhaustion I felt. I ran a bath in the tub, but didn't linger in the water even though it felt wonderful. I needed sleep.

Within seconds of collapsing on the bed, my hair still wet, I was out.

The next thing I was aware of was a far-away voice calling my name.

"Mother?" I mumbled. I turned on the bed, wondering if Lana and I had overslept.

This wasn't my bed. This wasn't my room at home. I gasped and sat up, blinking and disoriented.

"Maya, it's time to wake up. I've come to help you dress." It was Iris.

Everything came rushing back to me and I swallowed, trying to work some moisture back into my parched mouth.

"Dress for what?" I croaked.

"The ranks of favor, and then the party," she said. She held up a shimmering pale green gown. "To celebrate the end of the first phase of the Tournament. Lord Toric will be there."

I stared at her a moment as I tried to process what she was saying.

Lord Toric? I swung my legs over the side of the bed. Well,

it would be the perfect opportunity to tell him exactly what I thought of the way he sent Earthens to get torn apart by vicious forest creatures.

12

Toric

AS I'D WATCHED the first challenge of the Tournament of the Offered, my eyes had been drawn again and again to Maya. Inside, I was cheering her on. My heart soared at her every move that would win favor for her in the rankings.

The rankings. I grimaced at the memory of negotiating the first round.

After the Offered had completed their introductions and the Priestess, Akantha, and I were alone in the chamber under the throne, my mind churned as I searched for a way I could champion Maya without giving myself away to Akantha.

As the Mistress of Tournament, Akantha had to agree to the ranks of favor I proposed before they could become official. The Priestess, as the embodiment of the sacred texts, also had to agree, but it had become convention for the Priestess to go with the rankings the Lord set forth most of the time. As long as the Lord's reasoning for the rankings could be defended by passages from the sacred texts, the Priestess would not override the Lord's decision.

But the Priestess served another critical function in these proceedings. We would call upon her to break a standoff if—or more likely, *when*, with Akantha involved—the Mistress of Tournament and I could not reach agreement. This was my second Tournament with Akantha as Mistress of the event. The first, six months ago, had gone relatively smoothly, but even then I'd known she was testing the waters and wasn't yet trying to wield her power. Based on Akantha's increasing assertiveness, I suspected that our days of relative agreement had come to an end.

I'd faced Akantha and tried to appear at ease. "Kalindi was the clear winner for the women—her introduction was impeccable. And Amet for the men."

I wanted to choose Maya first, but it would be too obvious that I was attempting to favor her. By the interpretation of the sacred texts, there was no denying that Kalindi was the undisputed winner for the women's rankings.

Akantha nodded. "Agreed, my Lord. They're the obvious choices." Then her eyes gleamed, and I could tell she was already relishing the thought of arguing with me. "It's the next few spots in the females' rankings that will take some hashing out. Who do you favor, my Lord?"

I disagreed with her use of "females" and "males" when

referring to the Offered. Why couldn't she simply say "men" and "women?" I also hated the way she said "my Lord." It was always with her signature look—a slight twitch of her upper lip, the hint of a sneer. A look that reminded me of Jeric. Akantha got away with her sneering only because she seemed immune to insecurity and held power. Double power, in fact. The Mistress of Tournament *and* the favored lover of the brother of the Lord. If she figured out how to worm her way into any more power than she already had, I sincerely feared for the future of the Calistan race.

"Second . . ." I paused, pretending to think. "Meribel, perhaps. Or Maya." I looked steadily into Akantha's eyes, trying to remain composed while gauging her reaction to the mention of Maya.

Akantha's face tightened into a shrewd expression, and my heart dipped. Had she guessed?

She snorted a laugh. "The sacred texts do *not* support choosing Maya over Meribel for second place. Meribel's introduction was clearly superior." Her tone dripped with haughty confidence.

I knew she was right—Meribel had exuded the grace and devotion to the Lord's service that, though certainly not equal to Kalindi's, was superior to Maya's unusual introduction by the guidelines of the sacred texts.

But I looked to the Priestess, hoping she'd see something I'd missed. "I propose Maya for the rank of second," I said. I knew I should have left it, but I couldn't help myself.

"And I challenge for Meribel as second." Akantha voiced her formal objection to my proposal.

If the Priestess felt the performance of two Offered were more or less equal by the sacred texts, the Lord's choice was the default winner.

The Priestess sat very still for a moment, her gaze distant. "By the sacred texts, Meribel is more worthy."

Akantha gave a satisfied little hum and flipped a wave of brown hair over her shoulder. I bit back my disappointment, but I knew that I couldn't heavily vie for Maya again during this discussion. Even now, Akantha might already be suspicious.

I had to concede the third spot as well. But with a flash of triumph that I managed to hide, Maya was ranked fourth.

As I'd watched the Offered leave the throne room to enter the first official challenge of the tournament, the one Calistans informally called "the first culling," I hoped Maya's standing in the ranks of favor had provided her a boost of confidence. Given that she was untrained and had delivered an unorthodox introduction, her rank of fourth was a real accomplishment.

It was tradition for the Lord to throw a commencement party during the first challenge. The attendees—nobles, dignitaries, officials, celebrities, women of the harem, and the royal family—milled in small groups or sat at tables. The wine and brew flowed freely. I had to watch along with a few hundred others as live images of the Offered were projected onto the walls of the largest social room in the palace.

I wished more than anything to escape to the privacy of

my chambers so that I could observe the Tournament without worrying about masking my reactions, but it was my duty to be at the party. I stayed at the royal table as much as I could during the event. I was in no mood to entertain idle small talk and knew that most of the guests wouldn't approach me if I appeared to be in the middle of a meal or a conversation with one of the royals at my table.

When Maya nearly fell from the platform, I sucked in a breath and squeezed the armrests of my chair in a white-knuckled grip. A glance at the audience reassured me that everyone was transfixed on the action and no one had seen my slip. Except for one person: my sister Cassiopeia. She raised her brows at me, clearly curious. But Cassi wouldn't use what she saw to torment or betray me. She was not Jeric. In fact, she was so unlike Jeric it was difficult to understand how the two of them had come from the same set of parents.

I scratched the edge of my jaw with my right hand, and Cassi replied by tapping her left index finger to the side of her chin. I allowed myself the faintest grin at our childhood signals. When we were young, we'd devised these particular gestures to be the equivalent of wagging our tongues at each other. There had been times when we'd employed them so vigorously during royal dinners that we'd both gone to bed with bright red marks on our faces.

But with Cassi, things were always in good fun. Even our childhood bickering had usually ended in laughter.

My sister had often been my sounding board and

confidant. Perhaps I could confess to her something about my intense reaction to Maya? It might be safe. But certainly not here.

The culling challenges of the Tournament always turned my stomach. Not for the first time, I wished my father were still alive so I could ask him how he'd approached the Tournament. As the Calistan Lord, I was supposed to be the royal example of dedication to the sacred texts, and I believed that in nearly every way I was. But watching young Earthens die brought me no satisfaction, even though the culling challenges were required in the texts.

Some of the more fanatically devout attendees actually cried out praises when an Earthen Offered—Larisa, who'd fallen from the platform and been knocked unconscious—lost her life early in the challenge. And the ones who truly enjoyed bloodshed—Akantha and Jeric among them—often applauded or cheered the deaths, poorly masking their enjoyment behind insincere shouted quotations from the sacred texts.

During past Tournaments, I'd always managed to steel myself during the culling. I'd remind myself that this was the way of things, it had always been the way of things, and as Lord it was my duty to continue to uphold the way of things. While young Earthens died, I would repeat that thought over and over to myself. But this time, my heart lurched and pounded with every dramatic turn of events as the Offered fought for their lives.

As the late evening wore on, some of the attendees grew

tired and went home. But many stayed through the night and into the morning, partying as the Offered suffered injuries and fended off dangers in a wild forest of a neighboring planet under Calistan control.

Just before dawn, Cassi came to sit next to me. "How do you find these Offered, my Lord?" she asked. Her words were formal, but she leaned over, resting her elbow on the arm of my chair and propping her chin on her hand, grinning up at me in a girlish fashion.

"I find them as suitable as any others," I answered.

"And have you been entertained by this first challenge of the Tournament?"

"Entertained, yes, Lady Cassiopeia." If entertainment meant having my heart jump up my throat every few minutes, then I was certainly entertained. I couldn't help a quick glance up at the projection on the wall that was trained on Maya.

I reached for a goblet and sipped sweet wine. "How are you, Cassi?" I asked quietly, dropping any pretense of formality.

She sighed, but it was a sigh of contentment. "So well. So *very* well." She leaned in and bit her lower lip for a moment, her eyes sparkling. "We're expecting. I haven't even told Mother yet."

My lips parted in surprise, and then my surprise melted into joy. I gripped her hand, giving it a brief warm squeeze. "I'm so happy for you and Ralor."

I should have noticed that she had not partaken of any wine or brew all night. At any other Tournament, I'm sure I would have noticed, but tonight I'd been very distracted.

Cassi's eyes shone. All she'd ever wanted was to have a family of her own. She and Ralor had been married barely a year, but when it came to children they'd both been eager from the start. A part of me envied her. She'd married the man she loved, and she was starting the life she'd dreamed of since we were little.

"How are you feeling?" I asked.

"I need to get to bed, I'm absolutely exhausted. But other than that, I'm wonderful." A tinkling laugh escaped her lips. Then her expression grew wry. "Well, aside from all the vomiting. But even that can't get me down. I'm just so thrilled. And so is Ralor."

"I am thrilled, too. I quite like the thought of a little niece or nephew running through the palace hallways."

She tilted her head to one side. "What about you, brother? You are nearing the time of choosing a Calistan wife to bear your heirs. Then you'll have children of your own."

I shook my head and flicked my fingers back and forth as if shooing away a fly. "That is still months away."

"It will be here before you know it."

I took another sip of wine to avoid responding. At the age of twenty-eight, the Lord was obligated to take a wife. It wasn't a union of love like Cassi and Ralor's, but one of necessity. The Lord must bear children—at least one son, in particular—so that a new Lord would be ready to take his place if the Return to Earthenfell did not occur within his reign.

I was not eager to go through with the process. The woman had to be Calistan, and she had to be approved by the Council, High Priestess Lunaria, and the immediate members of my family. That meant Jeric would have a say, and the thought turned my stomach.

In many ways, it was a strange position to be in. The Lord's harem women would bear his children in the event of the Return and the reclamation of Earth. But as long as our enemies still attacked and we were bound to stay here on Calisto, more Calistan children in the bloodline of the Lord must be produced.

A shout went up, and I jumped and quickly scanned the projections. Had another Offered perished?

No—the sun was rising, and the challenge was almost over. But there was a commotion, and the stalwart revelers who still remained were all gathering under one projection.

It was the one trained on Maya and the others near her. And Maya was in trouble.

With my heart banging in my chest, I watched her fight. The giant carnivorous birds of the forest had surrounded her, but she wasn't giving up.

When three other Offered came to her aid, it took all of my strength to suppress the encouraging shout that threatened to burst from my throat.

A bead of sweat dripped down my temple as I watched, riveted.

When the portal opened, I cursed under my breath.

Akantha should have positioned it closer to the Offered. Instead, she'd placed it several yards away. She could have made it easier for them to escape—she had complete authority to do so. They'd survived the night, and they did not need one more test.

After Maya disappeared into the light of the portal, my shoulders dropped with relief and I began breathing again. One of the young men with her wasn't so lucky. I closed my eyes for a long moment as the unfortunate boy was dragged away. Akantha was at least partly responsible for his death, and I truly did not understand her cruelty.

But I couldn't help the new warmth that spread through me. Maya had made it. She'd survived. And she'd shown bravery, quick thinking, and benevolence toward her fellow competitors.

"Take care, Toric," Cassi whispered. In the tension of the final moments of the challenge, I'd nearly forgotten she was there. I turned to her, and her serious face cooled the glow of victory I felt for Maya's performance. "Do not betray your personal preference. Nothing good would come of it."

My face hardened, and I silently cursed myself. I did not have to be told of the danger, but I clearly had not concealed my feelings well enough if Cassi had detected them.

I nodded. "I know," I whispered back.

"WHAT SAY YOU, my Lord? Did Kalindi sufficiently meet your

favor during the culling to retain the honor of first place?" Akantha lounged a bit too casually on the divan, considering it was in my private receiving chamber. She twirled a strand of hair lazily around her finger, but I wasn't fooled. Akantha was always out for blood, even if it was just for the sport of it.

Kalindi had performed well, using a large section of the fallen platform as a shield under which to hide from the prowling, bloodthirsty tredaks. She and two young men had managed to survive there. But beyond figuring out a way to survive and allowing two of the young men to share her hiding spot, Kalindi had not displayed any exceptional valor.

I'd been debating with myself since the challenge ended a half hour ago. I believed Maya had performed well enough to take first place in this challenge, but strongly preferred that the suggestion came from someone other than me.

"I don't think so," I said. I leaned back and sighed deeply, interlacing my fingers at the back of my head. "I think at least one other outperformed Kalindi."

I flipped a glance at High Priestess Lunaria, who sat straight and still on a high-backed chair and wore her usual impassive expression.

Akantha tapped her pursed lips with the maroon-polished nail of her index finger. "Yes. I believe Maya far exceeded Kalindi in this challenge."

"I agree," I said, nodding my acquiescence as my heart soared. "Then so it is."

I started to turn to the Priestess to confirm her approval,

when Akantha sat up. "But what about Britta? She attempted to help others. She helped to save Maya's life toward the end," she said.

"Yes, but Maya equally saved Britta's by leading her to a better place to take cover," I shot back. "And before that, Maya warned all the others including Britta to run when the tredaks were coming to attack. She could have simply allowed the attack to happen, which would have culled more of her competition. It would have been a massacre if she hadn't shouted a warning."

Akantha grunted and waved her hand, but when she came back with no argument I felt a flash of triumph.

We briefly reviewed some of the actions of the other women, but hit no significant differences of opinion over their performances.

"I propose for this challenge the following order of rank," I said. "Maya, Britta, Kalindi, Meribel, Riki, Cheytan." The names of the dead women were left off the list.

Akantha nodded her agreement, and we both turned to the Priestess. She closed her eyes for several seconds.

"I find these ranks of favor in harmony with the sacred texts," she said.

I did the mental calculation and bit the inside of my cheek to suppress a grin. This wouldn't bump Maya into first place overall—Kalindi's points from the introduction still kept her in first place—but now Maya would be in second, just a point behind Kalindi.

As before, the men were easier to rank. Orion earned the top spot for this challenge, which moved him to the top overall by one point over Amet. I'd watched Orion and Maya work together in the forest, and it made me approve of the muscular young man even more. Amet was by far the more polished, but Orion possessed a simple sincerity that I liked. He reminded me of Victor in that way.

When our deliberations were complete, the two women left my chambers. I knew I should get to bed. It was dawn, and I was bone-weary from the late night and drained from the tension of the competition. I would need to rise in just a few hours for the daily session with the Council, followed by the announcement of the ranks of favor and then the celebration that traditionally came after the first challenge. But I paused at the small balcony that faced the sunrise, drawing a deep breath into my lungs and drinking in the warming colors of the sky.

Despite my fatigue, I felt enlivened. My entire body buzzed as if charged by some strange new infusion of energy.

"My Lord, do you require company when you retire?" Victor's voice came at my back.

I turned and considered for a moment, running through the faces of the harem women. "Darafina again."

He bowed his head, backed away three steps, and then left.

I stood under a hot shower for several minutes, allowing the heat to soak into my body. After drying myself, I walked naked into my sleeping chamber.

When I saw who was in my bed I stopped short, the muscles of my jaw flexing in irritation. "I did not call for you, Sytoria."

She lay on her side with the covers thrown back, one knee up. One hand gripped a set of bondage cuffs, and the other trailed slowly from her knee to her inner thigh.

Her eyes traveled partway down my body to my growing arousal, and her lips twitched into a knowing smile. "Perhaps you didn't, but I can see that you want me here all the same."

I lifted my chest and looked down at her coldly. "I command you to get out of my bed and leave my chambers."

Uncertainty flashed in her eyes. "My Lord, surely you don't mean—"

"Now," I cut her off.

She lay there for a moment, clearly shocked, and then slowly sat up, moved to the edge of the bed, and stood.

She straightened and squared her shoulders. "I know you, my Lord," she whispered. "And I know that it is only a matter of time before you will be calling for what only I can give you."

When I didn't reply, she finally turned and tossed the cuffs on the bed and stalked from the bed chamber, not even bothering to don her robe.

I locked the bedroom door behind her. I was in no mood for company now.

I fell into bed, and for once it felt good to be there alone. It felt deeply satisfying to have bested my desires. Even a few days ago, I probably would have succumbed to Sytoria's tricks and manipulation. But recently I'd begun to catch moments of peace like I hadn't experienced since I was a child, before I was kidnapped.

I fell asleep anticipating the next time I would see the dark angel.

13
Maya

AS I WAITED to enter the throne room with the other Obligates, I touched the bouncy waves at the back of my hair lightly with my fingertips. After Iris had helped me get into my dress—a lavish gown with a high-low hem that revealed my legs up to the tops of my knees in front and trailed along the ground behind my heels in back—a servant had come to fix my hair and makeup.

It was surreal to sit at a vanity and get done up like a princess only hours after fighting for my life and witnessing some of my fellow Obligates lose theirs. I'd watched in the mirror as the servant pulled the sides of my hair back in graceful twists and then created a flattering cascade of curls around my shoulders with her various styling tools, feeling distant from what was happening to me and around me.

I'd never looked like this in my life. With a pang of homesickness, I wished Mother could see me. My homesickness deepened tenfold when I thought of my sister. I longed to stay up late, whispering to Lana about Lord Toric, the other competitors, Akantha, Iris, and what it was like to be on Calisto. It was a physical ache, like ravishing hunger or the heartache of grief. I drew a deep breath and tried to pull myself into the moment.

Iris had told me that occasionally we would get to dress up like this, that it was an opportunity for Lord Toric to observe us in formal dress and social situations.

Akantha had made it clear that Obligates weren't allowed to chat with each other without permission, but I looked around for Orion and gave him a little wave. He and the other men were dressed in pressed black pants and shirts with collars. Just as the women's dresses were in different styles and colors to flatter each of us, the men's shirts were tailored to the wearer.

Orion nodded at me and winked. I nearly smiled back, for a moment imagining that we were on our way to a dance or fete back home.

Akantha's glare reminded me that this was no dance, and I was so far from home that it might as well not exist.

I tried to imitate the way Kalindi stood and moved in her high-heeled shoes. I'd worn Mother's only pair of high heels once, to my last school dance before I graduated, but they weren't nearly as high as the satin ones I wore now.

I couldn't understand how anyone could wear these shoes for more than a few minutes. I already felt pressure spots where blisters were sure to form before the day was done. Iris said that with practice I would become accustomed to the shoes, but I wasn't sure I cared to do that. Not that I really had a choice in such matters.

When I saw the line begin to move, I shifted my weight toward my toes and pulled my stomach muscles firm as Iris had coached me—she said it would help with my balance as I walked in the heels.

I had to focus on keeping my ankles from wobbling and not catching a heel on my dress as I walked, so it wasn't until I stopped in the middle of the throne room with the other Obligates that I was able to look up at Lord Toric.

He looked truly regal, wearing navy trousers and a shirt of the same silky fabric that crossed over in the front, revealing a V of bare skin at his upper chest. A simple cream-colored braided rope belt was wrapped a few times around his waist. The fabric of his clothes caught the light in a subtle, rich shimmer when he shifted.

As he surveyed us, his eyes moving slowly down the line of Obligates, my stomach dipped nervously. He looked very much a king, his jaw set and his eyes serious. When his gaze paused on me for a split second, my heart bumped. And when his eyes seemed to soften and warm a bit, my pulse flew away at a gallop.

I resisted the urge to press my hands against my stomach

to try to still the fluttering there. Was it my imagination? It felt as if he'd acknowledged me in a different way than the others, but I didn't trust that I'd read his look correctly.

Akantha said a few words to welcome the audience to the next phase of the Tournament, and then she turned with a flourish of one hand up at the wall.

When the tile with my face and name appeared at the top of the women's rankings for the forest challenge, I sucked in a shocked breath.

I'd received the highest rank of favor for the culling challenge.

I glanced at the men's board and saw that Orion had been ranked first as well, and a swell of pride warmed me.

Then the tiles flashed and began to rearrange themselves. Mine slid down to second place behind Kalindi's, indicating that she was still the overall leader. But I'd moved up two places in the overall ranks of favor. I could only stare at the tiles as Akantha made a few more general remarks to the audience.

I felt fifty pounds lighter when Akantha took us back through the door that led to our dressing rooms. When I went inside my room, Iris was already waiting for me on the divan. She stood and held out her arms, and I started to rush to her before I remembered the shoes. I quickly pulled the straps off my heels, kicked off the shoes, and let her fold me into an embrace.

"Well done, Maya." Her voice was warm and smiling as she gave me a squeeze.

"I can hardly believe it," I said breathlessly.

She let me go, and I sank to the divan.

"Okay." I tried to gather myself, knowing I couldn't afford to get distracted even by a victory. "What's next, and what can I do to stay near the top?"

"The party is not a formal challenge in the tournament, but make no mistake, you *will* be judged on your conduct, and it will figure in your rank somehow," Iris said. She sat down next to me, crossed her ankles, and smoothed her dress over her lap. "Lord Toric will keep in mind the impression you make at this event when he chooses the ranks after the next formal challenge."

I sat up straighter and folded my hands in my lap, trying to imitate Iris's posture and poise. "What about my conduct will he be evaluating?"

"Your charm. Conversation skills. If you have any talents you might use to entertain the party-goers, this would be the time to bring those out and let them shine."

I thought about Lana's singing. If only I had her voice. But I couldn't sing and there'd never been any money for instrument lessons. I couldn't help feeling deflated. "I don't have any special talents to put on display for a crowd. I guess I'll have to rely on other things."

"After Lord Toric arrives, be sure to stay where he can see you. You don't want to be difficult to find. He may not speak to all of the Obligates, but if he does speak to you, it's a good sign." Her eyes gleamed and a smile touched her lips. "And

I would put money on him seeking you out. He seems . . . intrigued by you. You must use that to your advantage."

My pulse skipped as I remembered how his gaze had lingered on me just now in the throne room. And before, during the introduction ceremony, when he'd quirked a tiny smile at me. So it wasn't just my imagination—Iris had noticed, too. "And what should I do or say when he speaks to me?"

"Expressing you desire to serve him is always a safe theme. Beyond that, let him see your best qualities. Remember, he wants gracious, honorable, intelligent, warm women around him—not just beautiful, charming ones, although beauty and charm are important too."

I was silent for several seconds as I clenched my hands together in my lap. The glow of my victory was quickly fading, and some of the anger and outrage I'd felt after the forest challenge was returning. "But what if I don't actually feel a desire to serve? What if I think this entire tournament is equally barbaric and ridiculous? I just watched my fellow Earthens die, Iris. And from what you told me, that was the very *purpose* of the challenge in the forest." I knew I should be practicing composure, that I shouldn't be airing these frustrations, but I couldn't hold them in. "The Calistans—Lord Toric—sent us out there with the intention that some would not survive. Why would I want to expend any effort kissing up to the Calistan Lord, pretending to want to serve him? I don't want to be here!"

I had to stop as my throat tightened and angry tears sprang

to my eyes. I bit down hard on my lips to keep from bursting into tears.

"There would be no Earthenfell home, no family, if not for the Calistans, remember?" Iris's eyes were steely, but her tone was not unkind. "This—you and the other Obligates—is the price they ask for keeping your family and your old home safe under the shield."

I took a shaking breath. "I know that. Of course I know that. But I'm still angry."

"This is what it means to make a sacrifice. And Maya," Iris's tone turned stern, and she waited until I looked up at her before continuing. "You *must* play the game. Anger against Lord Toric will not help you. You must do whatever it takes to earn favor and to win. Your life depends on it."

"You mean there are more culling challenges still to come?"

"There may be, that depends on the Mistress of Tournament and her decisions about the challenges, but . . ." Her mouth worked, as if she could not quite decide which words to choose next. When she spoke, her words came haltingly. "It's not—it's not just that. There are only—only *winners* in the Tournament. One young man and one young woman. You do not want to be one of the losers." She spoke the last sentence very slowly.

I stared at her, wide-eyed as a prickly sensation of foreboding crawled through me. "But I thought . . . I thought the losers were traded, sent to other alien worlds as slaves. Not that I would wish for that fate, but is that not . . .?"

She looked into my eyes for a very long moment. Then slowly, very deliberately, she lifted a hand and brought it to the back of her neck. Her implant. "I am forbidden from giving you any more details. But take this to heart, Maya." She leaned in close and fixed me with a deadly-serious stare. "*You do not want to be one of the losers.*"

My mouth went dry as fear began to twist my stomach, binding it tight. I gave her a slow wide-eyed nod.

"Now, while we still have a moment, let me instruct you on some basic social rules," Iris said, turning business-like.

She gave me guidelines about when and to whom to curtsy, rules about touching Calistans (I should not do it unless they initiated contact first), whether to walk next to or behind a Calistan (it depended on his or her royalty and standing), and questions that were safe to ask (small-talk topics were generally okay, but I should not speak about battles, religion, or anything to do with Earthenfell). I tried to push her warning to the back of my mind and focus on her instructions, but the knot in my stomach remained.

A chime sounded overhead, and Iris stood. "One more thing," she whispered quickly, eyeing the door, which was swinging open. My Calistan stylist walked in. "Stand strong and be proud of your performance so far and don't let the other Obligates rattle you."

My stylist flipped her fingers at me in an upward motion, indicating I should stand. With quick, expert movements she used some of her styling tools to touch up my hair and reapplied some of my makeup, and then she was gone.

"It's time." Iris gestured to the door.

I slipped my shoes back on, took a deep breath, and squared my shoulders.

I'd been planning to tell Lord Toric exactly what I thought of a competition where Calistans sent young Earthens to die. As desperately as I wanted to survive—and survival meant winning—pretending that I was thrilled to be here and ecstatic to be his slave was an act I doubted I could convincingly pull off. But now Iris's warning rang through my mind over and over like the somber toll of a bell. I wasn't sure *what* I would say when I came face to face with the alien Lord.

WITH AKANTHA IN the lead as always, the other Obligates and I followed her through corridors in a rustle of dresses and clicks of fancy shoes. Part of me had expected to be taken outside— on Earthenfell our fetes always took place in public squares and parks—but instead we ended up at a wide doorway within the palace. The room beyond was enormous, and I caught glimpses of gauzy curtains and lots of twinkling lights.

Akantha stopped and turned to us. "During this event, you are free to speak to each other. You're free to do *whatever* you'd like with each other, in fact." She raised an eyebrow and smirked. "And you may speak to the Calistans in attendance as well. Take your fill, Earthens. Your opportunities to indulge are very few. Enter the ballroom." She tilted her head toward the open doorway and waited for us to go in ahead of her.

That was about as close to kind as Akantha had been since our arrival on Calisto, but it didn't put me at ease. Something about her manner never failed to set my nerves on edge.

When I stepped into the ballroom, all of my anxieties temporarily fled, whipped away along with my breath. The *oohs* and *aahs* of the other Obligates echoed my own reaction.

The room literally glittered. Strings of crystals lined the walls, lights sparkled in cut glass chandeliers, and nearly everything else in the ballroom—sconces, cocktail tables, chairs, divans, side tables, even the gauzy curtains—was decorated with twinkling faceted stones.

The ceiling was vaulted, but the chandeliers hung low, not far over our heads, giving the room a surprisingly intimate ambiance for such a large space.

Calistan men and women milled about drinking from goblets, eating from small plates, and talking in groups. Some lounged on settees and chaises, or on giant pillows that were strewn about the floor. Many of them paused what they were doing to peer at us and then leaned into each other, whispering. My cheeks grew warm as I took in so many judgmental eyes on us.

"Akantha gave us permission to make merry," someone behind me said. I turned to see a bright smile on Kalindi's heart-shaped face. "I for one am going to live it up!"

She gathered the front of her skirt an inch or two off the floor, and with an excited little trilling laugh, she set off toward the nearest buffet table. She smiled and moved as if an entire room full of Calistans weren't scrutinizing her. And of course, as the first Obligate to break away from the group, all eyes followed her as she gracefully strode across the room with her head high.

I watched as she made little bowing nods at each Calistan she passed. And I watched how the Calistans reacted to her. Some raised their eyebrows in surprised but approving expressions. A few even nodded to each other, clearly pleased by what they saw.

Kalindi knew what she was doing, not that I'd really doubted it.

"I would like to try whatever they are offering." A resonant male voice said at my shoulder. I looked up at Orion. "How about you?"

I took a deep breath, gave him a grateful smile, and nodded. "Yes, we might as well. Shall we grab plates and goblets and then walk around a bit?"

I wanted to get a feel for the room, for the way the Calistans interacted. And, curiosity ate at me—I had to know if Lord Toric was yet in attendance.

I disliked the feeling of following in Kalindi's wake, but we'd have to pass right by the buffet table she'd gone to in order to get to any of the others, and I was afraid it would look like I was trying to hide if I went to one of the buffets toward the back of the room. Iris had said to stay visible.

I held my stomach muscles firm and took slow steps in my

heels. My toes were nearly numb from being pinched in the uncomfortable shoes during the trek from the dressing rooms to the ballroom. I could feel blisters forming, but I did my best to focus elsewhere.

"Are you okay?" Orion asked.

I cast him a questioning glance.

"You're walking strangely," he said.

I kept a smile on my face, but blew out a frustrated breath through gritted teeth. "It's these blasted shoes. I've never really worn high heels."

"I don't know how you walk in the things," Orion said with a sympathetic shake of his head. "But you do look beautiful."

"Thank you." I was surprised by how nice the compliment felt. Kind words were few and far between on Calisto. "You look very handsome. Oh, I should congratulate you on your rank! You are doing extremely well."

"As are you," he said. "And I would venture to say that your competition is by far the more difficult one."

I couldn't argue with that. But still, the stakes were the same for both of us.

"Do you know if he's here?" I said in a low voice. "Lord Toric?"

Orion shook his head. "Not yet. My guide told me he would arrive later."

When we reached the table, Orion handed me a plate and took one for himself. All manner of delectable fruits, tiny sandwiches, cheeses, meats, breads, and other savory treats spread out before us like some kind of fantastic food mirage. Again, I was struck by how strange it was to go from fighting for my life to this scene of comfort and luxury in a matter of hours.

My mouth was watering, but I didn't want to get too distracted by the party. This was a rare opportunity to speak with Orion. The last time we'd been given permission to talk to each other, we were too focused on staying alive to have any sort of useful conversation.

"Has your guide revealed anything to you? Anything you did not know before?" I asked quietly as we moved down the table, filling our plates.

Orion seemed to consider my question for a moment. "Yes, actually. He said that the Lord's Earthen manservants are allowed to, ah, mix with Calistan women."

I looked up at him sharply. "Really? That surprises me."

"Me to," Orion said with a short laugh. "What have you learned?"

"My guide told me that the harem is not just for serving the pleasure of the Lord. In the event that the enemies are defeated and the Lord can lead the Return of the Calistans to Earthenfell, the harem will bear his children there."

He gave me a wide-eyed look, and his hand paused over a stack of sweet rolls. "That is . . . not at all what I expected you to say."

"I know," I said. "Makes me wonder what else we don't know. And there's something important, something that my guide is not allowed to say to me. It's about what happens to the Obligates who lose the Tournament. She couldn't tell me, but she seemed to be saying that the losers are not handled the way we've always been led to believe. It's something far worse, if I understood what she was implying." My stomach knotted again at the memory of Iris's face as she'd tried to convey to me the importance of emerging the winner of the Tournament.

His eyebrows drew down in a troubled expression. "I had begun to wonder about that myself. It's very distressing. As if we don't already have enough to be anxious about. Still, it doesn't really change our goal. The best outcome for both of us was, and still is, to win."

Other Obligates had followed us to the buffet, and for a moment I wondered if I should ask Britta or maybe Meribel what they knew. But the truth was I really didn't trust any of them except Orion.

I looked for Kalindi and spotted her sitting primly on the edge of a settee not far away almost in the exact center of the room. She smiled and nodded at the Calistans who passed her, as if we were at an Earthenfell fete and this was the most fun she'd ever had. If Kalindi's guide had advised her to stay visible as Iris had done with me, Kalindi was doing a spectacular job.

A Calistan man stopped in front of Kalindi, and after she rose to curtsy, they chatted. After a moment, he went to one of the drink tables and then returned to her with two goblets and handed her one of them. He perched on the settee next to her.

A pair of Calistan men passing by slowed, and when she

smiled at them, they stopped. Again, she stood to curtsy.

Orion and I moved away from the buffet with our plates, and I eyed Kalindi as I ate one of the tiny sandwiches. It had some sort of creamy spread and slices of fresh-tasting crisp vegetables, the flavors and textures perfectly balanced.

"Shall we go sit over there?" Orion tipped his head at an unoccupied narrow bench with a low table in front of it that was several yards away. "We will have a decent view from that spot, and you can rest your feet for a few minutes."

"That's a wonderful idea." I was doing my best to walk gracefully, but all I really wanted to do was pull off my shoes and drop them in the nearest waste bin.

"The Calistan men are watching you," Orion said, tilting his head toward me so he could whisper.

I glanced at him and gave a little shake of my head. "They seem very much interested in Kalindi."

"Some of them are drawn to her, yes. But many more are watching you."

I glanced around, suddenly self-conscious. Was he right? Many of the Calistans *were* watching me and Orion, I now realized, but I was sure it was simply because Earthen Obligates were a curiosity to them. I tried to carry myself as if I were completely accustomed to attending extravagant parties in alien palaces.

My attention had so far been occupied by the main open part of the room, but along the sides there were thin veils of curtains creating semi-private little spaces.

I glanced into one as we passed and let out a shocked gasp. A Calistan man was sitting on a settee, and a Calistan woman sat astride him and they were kissing each other passionately. As if that wasn't startling enough, I realized the top of her dress had been pulled down, and part of her chest was bare. It was all I could do to keep from letting out shocked exclamation when I saw the man groping her breast. Heat bloomed up my face and chest.

My plate tipped in my hand, and a melon ball rolled off and plopped on the floor. Orion had bent down to pick it up in his napkin, but I was sure he'd looked into the curtained space, too.

"Does that shock you, Earthen?" I knew the voice before I turned to see Akantha standing at a cocktail table nearby. She gave me a heavy-lidded, insincere smile. Another Calistan woman and two men who were with her stared openly at me and Orion. The men's eyes locked on me, and I tried not to shrink under their gazes. "If you find *that* shocking, you have no place in Lord Toric's harem."

A nauseating combination of embarrassment and alarm coursed through me, and my cheeks burned even hotter.

With his hand at my elbow, Orion angled me away from Akantha and the amorous couple.

"That was . . ." I shook my head, unsure how to finish the sentence.

"Unexpected?" Orion offered.

"Yes. To say the least." I tried to pull myself together. My mind whirled, clamoring for a change of topic. "So . . . What is the point of this party for the male Obligates? How do you win Lord Toric's favor here?"

"When he arrives, I will be assigned to one of the royal men. I'll be his personal servant for the remainder of the evening."

I wrinkled my nose and pushed out my bottom lip in an exaggerated pout. "I only get you for a little while?"

His cheeks and the tips of his ears reddened slightly, and he looked pleased that I wanted his company. He gave me a little bow. "I'm at your service until then."

I sat down with our plates, and Orion went to get us drinks. I searched for Kalindi, but the place where she'd been sitting was now occupied by a pair of Calistan women.

A little musical flourish sounded behind me, and I twisted to find its source. About a dozen Calistans were gathered around a piano. When one of them shifted, I caught a glimpse of Kalindi's golden hair. She was at the piano. I suppressed a sigh. Only an Obligate with a training budget could have afforded years of piano lessons back on Earthenfell.

I set down my plate and rose, drawn by the music and the need to see how much approval her playing was garnering for her. Again, I cursed my lack of vocal talent. A beautiful voice like Lana's required no expensive instrument lessons.

I stood at the edge of the growing crowd around the piano. The Calistan men near me began turning around, peering at me as if I'd marched up and announced myself. Their expressions ranged from curious to a sort of hunger that made me draw back half a step.

I looked past the crowd to see Kalindi narrowing her eyes at me, clearly irritated that I'd taken attention away from her performance.

I shrank back a little, my heart tapping nervously. I should have stayed on the bench and waited for Orion. I tried to take another step back, but my heel caught. I attempted to right myself, but my heel was tangled in the back hem of my dress. I pulled at the fabric, which only served to upset my already-precarious balance. My ankle wobbled, and as if in slow motion I felt myself tipping.

No, no, no. I could not fall flat on my face. Not here. Not now.

A hand caught my arm just above my elbow and steadied me. I let out a relieved breath, and turned to thank Orion. But my words died on my lips as my gaze moved up a broad chest to the face towering over me. It wasn't Orion who'd helped me. It was a Calistan man.

Somehow remembering that I was supposed to be making a good impression, I managed to smile and incline my head. "Thank you for catching me. If not for your quick reflexes, I'm afraid I'd be sitting in a heap on the floor right now."

Something about the man's eyes looked familiar, but I didn't recall seeing him before. He bent to free my heel from the hem of my dress and then straightened. I had to tip my head back to see into his face. After a brief moment of hesitation I quickly curtsied, keenly aware of my own fumbling. But he didn't seem to mind. Or perhaps he was just too polite to react to my awkwardness.

"May I escort you to a seat? You look as if you could use a sip of water." He touched the back of my elbow and steered me away from the crowd around the piano.

"Yes, and thank you again." I gave him a grateful nod. "The air *is* quite dry here compared to Earthenfell, and I find I always feel a bit parched. I suppose it doesn't feel that way to you, though."

I felt more than a little idiotic at making such inane small talk, but the man didn't seem to mind. In fact, the corners of his lips stretched into a slow smile, as if I'd just delivered a delightful quip.

"The air here is actually quite sterile of the moisture and aromas you're used to," he said.

"Yes, that's exactly the impression I had when I arrived here," I said. Then I winced, realizing my words might have sounded critical. "Though please don't take my observation as complaint. Calisto certainly has its beauty. I caught a bit of the sunset, and it was absolutely lovely. And the palace is very impressive."

My heart dipped nervously when I realized where he was taking me—to one of the curtained areas. But he pulled two chairs to the edge of the space where we'd be able to see into the greater part of the room.

"Please, sit." He placed his hand on the back of one chair.

"I will get you some water."

I nodded my thanks. After he walked away, I surveyed the party, curious about what the others were doing. Meribel was speaking with her hands clasped at her waist, and a small crowd of Calistans had gathered around her. It looked as if she might be reciting poetry.

Britta was at one of the drink tables. She tipped a goblet back, rapidly emptying it, and then held it out to be refilled and drank deeply again. By the way she tottered a little when she moved away, I imagined she'd already made a couple of previous stops at the wine tables.

When the Calistan man returned, I took the cup he offered. He sat down on the chair next to mine and angled his body toward me, giving me a tilted gaze. The intensity in his eyes made me want to squirm.

After a few seconds, the silence began to feel awkward.

"I apologize," I said. "I should have introduced myself. I'm Maya."

"Yes, I remember," he said. "My name is Jeric."

"Were you in attendance at the Obligate introduction ceremony, Sir Jeric?" I asked.

"As the Lord's brother, yes, I most certainly was," he gave a short laugh.

"Oh! I didn't realize. I apologize for my ignorance. We Obligates are not made familiar with the royal family. We're not really told much, in fact." I'd let the last comment slip out under my breath, and I cast him a rueful glance, again feeling a little silly. "I'm honored to be in your company, Sir Jeric."

So this was Lord Toric's brother. That's where I'd seen those eyes before. Jeric bore a vague resemblance to the Lord, though in my observation he did not have the same regal, magnetic quality. But it couldn't hurt my chances to try to ingratiate myself to someone so close to the Calistan Lord.

"And do you have any other siblings?" I asked.

"Yes, a sister. Her name is Cassiopeia." He scanned the room and then nodded. "There, see the woman in pink with dark hair? That's Cassi."

She was too far away for me to discern whether she looked like her brothers, but I made a mental note of who she was.

"Do you have siblings?" he asked.

I glanced up at him, surprised that he would bring up the topic of the family I'd been ripped away from—that the traditions of *his* people had ripped me away from. For a split second, I bristled. Then I told myself that the smarter reaction was to assume that he was sincerely interested, possibly even sympathetic.

"I have a twin," I said. "Her name is Lana." I tried to keep a pleasant expression, but felt my smile faltering.

"A twin . . . two of you," he said, his tone oddly wondrous. The intent look on his face was disconcerting, and I shifted in my seat. "You must miss her terribly."

"I do, more than I could ever describe." My throat welled, cutting off any more words. I stared down into the cup I held.

I felt him watching me. He leaned closer, and when I

turned to him, I couldn't help a little flinch. His face loomed only inches over mine.

"I believe I could find a way for you to contact her," he said. His eyes gleamed. "But you can't tell anyone. If you tell, the consequences for both of us will be extremely grave, and you'll surely never speak to Lana again."

My heart leapt, but a wisp of skepticism followed. I gave him a sharp look. "Obligates are not allowed to communicate with anyone on Earthenfell."

"We call you Offered, not Obligates. Obligates is the Earthen term," he said absently. His focus seemed to have shifted to something across the room.

I frowned in confusion at his abrupt change of subject. Before I could formulate a question about how I would get to speak to Lana, Jeric muttered under his breath, clearly irritated about something. A second later, two Calistan men towered over us. My pulse jumped at their sudden appearance.

They were giving Jeric nearly identical flinty looks. "Clear out," one of them said. "By the order of the Lord."

Jeric's eyes darkened as his expression transitioned from irritated to angry. He glared at each man in turn, and then slowly rose from his seat. He straightened the front of his shirt with a sharp tug and then turned to me.

With a smile that failed to touch his eyes, he bent over me in a formal bow, grasped the fingers of my right hand, and planted a kiss just behind my knuckles. "It was my pleasure to make your acquaintance, Maya. I regret that I must leave you now, but our paths will surely cross again."

Then, with his back blocking the view of the two guards, he gave me a secretive little smile. "I will come for you so you can speak to Lana," he said at barely a whisper. He let go of my hand and touched the side of his index finger to his lips. "Remember—do not breathe a word to anyone."

I wanted nothing more than to shrink back from his gaze, which bored into me. His demeanor was gallant, but something about his manner felt threatening.

With wide eyes I nodded, unable to come up with any appropriate response before he disappeared around one of the curtains.

As soon as Jeric was gone, another tall figure appeared in front of me. For a second I thought Jeric had returned, but when I looked up, Lord Toric's blue-green gaze—so similar to his brother's and yet so very different—seemed to pin me to my chair and still my breath. The alien Lord did not look happy.

Just behind Lord Toric's left shoulder, Akantha's slitted eyes glared down at me.

The Calistan woman who stood with Akantha in the throne room—the Priestess—was at Lord Toric's other side, her face unrevealing.

My mouth went dry as I stared up at them.

14

Toric

I ENTERED THE ballroom with the Priestess, both of us walking behind Calvin and Palovich and a handful of Calistan nobles trailing behind us. I immediately sensed Maya among the swirl of energetic auras of the Earthens in attendance. She was somewhere midway back, near the left wall.

I'd intended to make my way slowly around the room, but something shadowy bristled through Maya's energy like a ghostly intruder, driving me to move straight to her instead of taking my time.

Calistans bowed as I passed, and the young Offered gaped at me with widened eyes before sinking into bows and curtsies. The nobles who'd entered with me dispersed to find the Offered men who were assigned to them for the evening, as a test of their skills of service. But I was only partially aware of these things as I sought out Maya.

The one thing that did distract me from Maya was Akantha, when she spotted me and left her table to join my little entourage. It was an unfortunate rule of the Tournament proceedings that she and High Priestess Lunaria were required to be in attendance when I interacted with the Offered men and women in events that figured into the rankings, even the ones that weren't formal Tournament challenges. The company of the Priestess I appreciated, but Akantha was a splinter in my thumb that had worked itself too deep for extraction.

When I came into view of Maya and I saw my snake of a brother sitting next to her, his body curved toward her and his eyes locked on her face, a searing wave of anger pulsed through me. My hands clenched, and I took a step forward but then stopped myself. It was not the time or place for a confrontation with Jeric, not with so many eyes watching.

"Get rid of him," I said through gritted teeth to my guards.

Akantha let loose a string of curses under her breath, and I shot her a glance over my shoulder and felt a little welling of satisfaction at her aggravation. By the look on her face, she was nearly as unhappy to see Jeric with Maya as I was. Akantha would likely make my brother pay for it later, but I had no sympathy for him.

When Jeric rose and then kissed Maya's hand, my anger flared again. Every muscle in my body strung tight. He shot me a smug, heavy-lidded look as he passed, and it was all I could do to stay where I stood.

"She's very special," he said to me, smiling darkly.

I managed to not give him the satisfaction of a reaction, but anxiety stirred through my anger. Of all the Earthen women, he'd singled out Maya and it gave me a deep feeling of unease.

I turned to Maya, who had not spotted me yet. Her eyes were huge, and she looked around dazedly, obviously agitated.

Jeric. He'd done or said something to her.

I swallowed back my fury and forced the tension from my muscles. It wouldn't calm her agitation if I seemed irate.

The flash of alarm in her eyes when she looked up at me suggested that I hadn't masked my ire toward Jeric well enough.

She stared in surprise for only a moment before she composed herself, rose, and sank into a deep curtsy. Her energy signature washed over me like a seductively fragrant evening breeze.

As much as I wanted to hide away with her among the curtains, I needed to put her at ease. I darted a furtive glance to each side, looking for something suitable. Four of the palace's most talented musicians were set up near the piano, waiting for someone—Kalindi, I recognized—to finish the piece she was playing.

"Please rise," I said to Maya. "I would very much like for you to accompany me, the Priestess, and the Mistress of Tournament to listen to the royal quartet."

Maya's eyes flitted nervously to Akantha, but then Maya

smiled at me, and my heart seemed to falter for a second under her blue-eyed gaze. "Yes, of course it would be my honor, my Lord."

She still seemed a bit rattled from the last few minutes' events, but I thought I read genuine gratitude in her eyes. Part of me was thankful that etiquette dictated she walk a step behind my left elbow. If she were beside me, I surely would have made a fool of myself staring at her. But another part of me hated that she was out of my line of sight, even if only slightly. Jeric had moved off into a group of nobles, but his presence still aggravated me and made me want to surround Maya with a wall of guards.

Rows of chairs had been set up in a curve around the music area. I went to the empty front row, which was always reserved for me, and gestured with an open hand at a chair. She stood in front of it, but did not sit until I did. So far, despite her nerves, she'd remembered her guide's etiquette instructions well.

She sat to my right, radiating that complex signature of energy that was uniquely hers. Akantha stepped ahead of the Priestess to take the seat to my left, where Akantha sat rigidly, clearly still seething over Jeric's attention to Maya. Not far away, my brother was studiously avoiding the darting glares Akantha kept shooting his way.

Kalindi finished her piece, and I joined in the small crowd's polite applause. She rose gracefully from the piano bench and placed one had on the edge of the piano to give a little curtsy. When she looked up and noticed me in the audience, she blushed prettily and gave me a deeper curtsy.

Though she did not affect me in the unique way Maya did, I could not help but admire Kalindi's training and natural grace. Her every movement and expression were nearly perfectly formed. I couldn't deny that even now she matched or even surpassed many of the women in my harem.

I felt Maya's eyes flitting to me and then away, and I turned to her. "How are you enjoying the celebration so far?" I asked. It took all of my willpower to resist staring at her, examining her every feature greedily.

"The food is wonderful, and the ballroom is breathtaking," she said. She shook her head and blinked a couple of times. "It's like a dream." Despite her enthusiastic words, her expression clouded. But she quickly recovered with a serene smile.

She looked up into my face, and my breath caught. The play of light emphasized the angles of her face, creating shadows over her eyes and darkening the slight hollows below her cheekbones, and it was if I'd caught a glimpse of what she would look like eight or ten years from now. After she'd discovered the dark, bold parts of herself that I'd sensed when I'd first seen her from my balcony.

She swallowed and licked her lips. "Will you be staying to enjoy yourself for the rest of the evening, or will your duties take you away early?" Her eyes flicked down to my waist and seemed to linger there for a moment.

I gave myself a mental shake. I should not be staring at her dumbly, expecting her to carry the conversation.

"This is the only thing on my agenda for the rest of the night," I assured her.

Her lips parted as if to respond, but then she hesitated for a moment. "My Lord, may I—may I ask you about the belt you wear?" she said, clearly uncertain about her query.

"Please." I tilted my head in interest. I couldn't imagine what she might have to say about my clothing.

"Did it come from Earthenfell?"

My brows rose a fraction. She was treading close to a taboo subject—the Offered were not supposed to inquire about Earthenfell. But her inquiry was not really about her home, not exactly.

"In fact, it did," I said. "And now you have me curious. How did you know?"

"I believe my sister may have been the weaver," she said. The warmth in her voice was steeped in sadness, betraying her deep feelings for her sister.

My mind reeled as sympathy poured through me. Dark memories of being taken from my family when I was a boy mixed with the heady sensation of Maya's energy in such close proximity, and for a moment I felt too light-headed to respond.

I blinked hard, pulling myself into the present moment. "If so, she is very talented. I own many similar pieces that were clearly made by skilled hands." A slow, warm smile spread over my face. For reasons I couldn't explain, the idea that I'd been wearing belts made by Maya's sister for years before I'd learned of Maya's existence delighted me.

The sadness melted from Maya's eyes, and her smile seemed to echo mine. "She is indeed talented." She gave a pleased little laugh. Then she looked up at me ruefully. "It is my misfortune that although my sister and I are identical twins, she seems to have ended up with the larger share of talents."

Her eyes widened, and she inhaled sharply through her nose, obviously regretting that she'd let that bit of self-criticism slip out. It wasn't a glaring misstep, but neither was it the elusive blend of humility and self-assurance that were the ideal for harem women.

Akantha let out an exasperated sigh at Maya's comment, but I couldn't help a soft chuckle. Maya was not following a script or taking on any affectation, and it was refreshing.

I tried to reassure her with both my eyes and my words. "You are currently second in the rank of favor, which certainly demonstrates that you possess talent."

It was a compliment, and certainly meant as one, but her face and energy darkened suddenly. The muscles of her jaw tightened as she fought to hold the smile on her face even as her eyes hardened. Her posture became wooden, and she turned her gaze away.

We had started to build a connection, and just like that, the invisible bridge between us vanished, and she felt as remote from me as the farthest star.

My heart lurched in my chest, and I searched for something to say that would close the gap that had suddenly expanded between us, but my mind remained stubbornly blank. And then the quartet started up, and I lost my chance to speak.

Sitting through the first piece with Maya stone-like next to me was torture. When it finally ended and the musicians took a break to re-tune their instruments, I turned to her. But before I could speak, Akantha's voice scraped across my eardrums.

"My Lord," Akantha said, her tone dripping with undisguised annoyance. "Don't you think it best to move on now and converse with the other ones? You've already devoted an inordinate amount of time to this one."

"Soon." I turned and drilled her with an unfiltered glare, but kept my voice mild so as not to alarm Maya. "Right now I would like Maya's continued company while we sample the food and drink."

Akantha's eyes flashed darkly, and her cheeks flushed in splotchy patches. "As you wish." She all but spat the words at me.

Her lack of respect was growing more blatant, and I would need to do something about it. But I needed to focus on Maya.

Passing through the bows and curtsies from the attendees, I led Maya to the largest buffet table. She was handling herself well, I thought, considering that nearly everyone in the room was watching us.

"My Lord, I have a message for you," a business-like voice said behind me, and I turned in surprise. "Your presence is required in the war room. The presence of the Priestess as well."

Catching the tone of urgency behind the messenger's

summons, my pulse quickened.

Stifling a sigh of regret, I looked down at Maya. "I apologize that I must depart to attend to some unexpected business. But please, continue to enjoy yourself." As much as I hated the idea of leaving her, especially with Jeric in the room, I had to go.

Maya's lips parted in a little O of surprise. "I regret that you must depart, too, my Lord." She hastily placed her plate on the edge of the buffet table and curtsied.

I turned to the messenger. "Go to the master of the guard and have him send one of my elite guards to meet me at the war room immediately." I was supposed to have two elite guards with me at all times, but I couldn't bring myself to leave Maya with Jeric. Perhaps it was petty of me, and maybe an overreaction, but Calvin was going to stay right here with her.

I walked a few paces with Calvin and Palovich right on my heels, waiting until we were out of Akantha's earshot. I turned to Calvin. "Stay here and make sure my brother does not bother Maya again tonight. And escort her back to her room at the end of the evening. I instructed the messenger to send a second guard for me right away."

I could tell that Calvin wanted to protest my leaving the ballroom with only Palovich—Calvin was a stickler for following the law, especially when it came to my protection—but I turned on my heel before he had the chance.

With the Priestess drifting along beside me like a spirit in her pale robes and Palovich striding behind us, we quickly moved through the corridors.

"What do you think it could be?" I asked the Priestess. I'd known her since before she was ordained, long before she rose to High Priestess in the Temple of the Mother Earth. Her name used to be Laurel before she surrendered her identity to her calling.

"I believe the tide is turning in our battles," she said quietly.

I nearly stumbled over my own feet as I gave her a sharp look, wondering how she could make such a guess. She did not say if the tide was turning for better or worse, but either way it was a momentous statement. We'd been battling for Earthenfell for many hundreds of years, and though there were small victories and defeats along the way, it had been centuries since there was a major shift in the momentum of the war.

My heart raced at the possibilities. By the time we reached the war room, I was literally breathless with anticipation.

Palovich stayed outside the door as the Priestess and I went in. The main feature of the circular war room was a large round table that could seat two dozen. But there were only four people who stood waiting for us—my mother, Master of War Xavier, Xavier's first in command, and the Head of Council.

The three men greeted me with a chorus of "My Lord" and nearly identical half-bows.

The largest wall monitor was already illuminated. It displayed a familiar graphic, one which reported the status of every battle in the war by location. A section that had been red for many months—indicating that we were losing ground— was now white. In fact, several sections that had long been red were now white.

White meant victory.

There were still many other battles that were red, and a good number that were green which indicated they were going in our favor. But in my lifetime we had scored only one major victory, and it was back when my father was still Lord.

I stared at the monitor, counting again to make sure I had it right. "Seven victories?" I turned to Xavier for confirmation, making no effort to disguise my shock.

"You are correct, my Lord." Triumph shone in his eyes.

I'd have to check the records to be sure, but I believed that seven battles won made Xavier the most successful Master of War in Calistan history.

I shook my head. "So suddenly? All at once like this?"

Part of me felt that I should be whooping in celebration, but I still hadn't overcome my disbelief.

"A series of very fortunate events combined with several strategic moves made by our forces seemed to culminate at the exact right moment," Xavier said. "The complete sequence will be detailed in tomorrow morning's war report."

"A massive victory, Master Xavier." I inclined my head in homage to his prowess. The Guardian Lord of Calisto and Earth was subject to no one and nothing except for the sacred texts, but Xavier had earned my deepest esteem. "How does this figure into the larger war to reclaim Earthenfell?"

"The coming weeks and months will tell us whether this is simply one very large step forward, or if it is the beginning of an unstoppable momentum," Xavier said. "Of course we will pour every resource and effort into ensuring it is the latter."

The room went silent, but I was certain that every one of us was thinking the same thing. The possibility that we would live to see the Return had become a glimmer on the horizon. Even the tiniest chance of it was nothing short of a miracle.

My mother was looking at me with eyes full of pride and shining with emotion. If these victories were indeed signs that the Return was near, her son would be the Lord to lead the long-awaited reclamation of our ancestral home. She stepped close to me and reached up to briefly place her hand on my cheek. I gave her a quick smile.

But we could not make assumptions, even in the glow of such news.

"This is a tremendous day for Calisto," I said. "We will need to address the nation. Congratulations, Master Xavier, on this immense step toward victory."

Though the Priestess had said nothing during the entire exchange, her usual serenity seemed somehow charged through with agitation. I needed to speak with her alone.

"I must excuse myself to my prayer room now, to contemplate this momentous change of events and ask for our further good fortune," I said. "Priestess, would you do me the honor of joining me in prayer?"

"Of course, my Lord," the Priestess said.

A flash of disappointment passed over my mother's face. I knew she wanted to talk about the victories, about the future, but I would have to appease her later. I squeezed her hand. "We will speak soon, Mother."

"Yes, my son," she said.

I kissed her cheek and turned to go.

Outside the war room, an experienced guard named Tullock had joined Palovich. They fell in step behind me and the Priestess for the silent walk to my chambers.

Two more guards stood outside the main entrance to my chambers, and Tullock and Palovich accompanied us inside and then stationed themselves on either side of the door.

"Priestess, please join me in my prayer room." I gave her a slight inclination of my head, which she returned.

We passed through the formal entryway of my private chambers, a receiving room, through the short hallway to my bed chamber, and then into my prayer room. Once we were in the tiny space with the door closed, I turned to her.

"This is unprecedented. I hardly trust that I can believe it's true. I ask for your wisdom and guidance, High Priestess Lunaria," I said. I kept my voice low, as if someone might be listening at the door, even though I knew we were safe here.

My heart pounded an anxious rhythm. I could tell by the Priestess's demeanor that she was similarly stirred.

She drew a deep breath and then sank to my prayer mat, sitting cross-legged and settling her opalescent robes around her. I sat too, facing her in the same posture.

"My Lord," she said. "You know I cannot see the future. My wisdom comes from the sacred texts, meditation, and prayer.

Not from any facility for soothsaying."

I nodded, wondering why she felt the need to preface with such statements.

"However," she continued, "we are most certainly on the threshold of a new day in our battle for Earthenfell and the right to return to our homeland in peace. The victories you just learned of are the start. I am certain of it."

Detecting the conflict in what she'd just said, I gave her a narrow-eyed look. "How do you know this?"

She looked intently into my eyes, and her fingers flexed in the folds of her robes. "There is another volume of the sacred texts. A secret one."

My mouth dropped open as I stared at her. I was positive I'd never heard mention of secret volumes. "Who else knows of this?"

She shook her head. "I don't know. I only became aware of it recently. On the day of the Selection, shortly after the new Offered arrived on Calisto."

"How did you learn of it?"

"It was delivered to me along with some inconsequential items I had ordered."

I blinked several times. "I don't understand. Who sent it? How do you know it is genuine?"

"I am making inquiries to try to discover who supplied it, and so far I have come up empty. But I do know that it is genuine. I can only guess that there is someone somewhere who holds a secret position of responsibility. Perhaps even within my own Temple. And somehow he or she knew this was the time to reveal the new volume to me." She seemed reluctant to say more, but after a moment she continued. "My Lord, it contains a sort of map for taking us back to Earthenfell."

I gaped at her again, unable to form a suitable response as a sudden chill walked up my spine and brought goose bumps to my arms.

She shifted and an agitated frown passed over her face. "Perhaps map is not the correct word to use. It is not that specific. But it is clear that as High Priestess I am to be the guide in this process."

"But we always knew that would be the case, that the High Priestess would facilitate the Guardian Lord in leading the Calistans back to Earthenfell," I said, finally finding my voice.

"It is probably not quite how you imagined," she said. "It is certainly not exactly as *I* had imagined. It is important that I have a hand in the process but not too strong a hand."

I squinted, giving her a sidelong look from the corners of my eyes. "You must guide things to try to ensure that certain events take place but without forcing these events or exerting undue influence?"

She nodded.

My gaze drifted and my eyes lost focus. "So it is not simply a matter of defeating our enemies, packing up, and shipping off to Earthenfell."

She gave a short laugh. "There seems to be a bit more to it than that."

I searched her smooth face. Though her expression was serene, there was a new tightness in the set of her jaw and a sharpness in the way her gaze flicked over my face.

A vague sense of foreboding circled around in the center of my chest. "Has something already gone off track?" I asked.

Dead silence filled the prayer room for a couple of seconds.

"Not yet, but I fear it will," she said. "One of the Earthen women—the one who must win this Tournament to keep us on the path back to our homeland—is in danger. If she loses the Tournament or if the wrong person uses her as a pawn, we will lose our chance at Earthenfell in our lifetimes. Perhaps forever."

My blood seemed to slow and freeze in my veins.

Maya.

The Priestess had to be speaking of Maya. I'd left Calvin to watch over her and see her back to her quarters, but I hadn't instructed him to stay. I'd need to set a guard outside her door around the clock. Surely that type of protection would not be against the sacred texts?

I couldn't seem to catch my breath. "I assume that as before, we can't directly interfere with the Tournament."

"No, we must not," she said sharply. "Our interference, even if well-meaning, could destroy everything. And the Earthen women must *not* find out that our fate rests with one of them. No one must learn of this."

I shook my head, trying to absorb everything I'd learned in the past few minutes. "Your new sacred text could have spelled out an easier way for us." I gave a short laugh.

Her face softened into a tiny, wry smile. "But the easiest path is never the one that leads to the greatest reward, my Lord."

A new, pure white light of purpose seemed to have ignited within me. I took in the wonder and hope in her eyes, and it dawned on me that our every action, our every move in the coming weeks, would steer the fate of our people.

15

Maya

I BERATED MYSELF as Lord Toric swept out of the ballroom with the Priestess. That was my chance to say how cruel this was, how terrible the practice of sending Earthens to their deaths, but I hadn't. I'd just smiled and chatted and made nice with him, and I hated myself for it.

"I guess he had something more important to do after all," Akantha said. I whipped around to find the Mistress of Tournament looming over me, and the hate in her eyes forced me back half a step. She plucked a grapeberry from a tray and popped it in her mouth and then shooed at me with the backs of her hands while she chewed. "Go on, now. Go find one of those Earthen boys, take one behind a curtain and give him a little thrill. Maybe that muscled one who fancies you. He looks innocent enough. He probably wouldn't last half a minute."

She threw her head back and gave a throaty laugh as she turned her back on me and walked away, her hips swinging seductively.

I pressed my lips together, pinching my mouth tight to hold in the words I wanted to fling at her. Why was she so cruel? She already had so much power over me and the other Obligates and obviously delighted in bossing us around. I didn't understand why she had to be so haughty.

I watched as she went to Lord Toric's brother, Jeric. The other Calistans at Jeric's table slinked away, leaving just the two of them. Akantha's entire body was rigid as she lit into Jeric. What had her so riled, I couldn't guess, and I was too far away to hear.

My eyes flicked to one of Lord Toric's guards, who had stayed behind when the alien Lord left the ballroom. Although the guard stayed a respectful distance away and didn't look at me in any overt way, I couldn't help feeling that he'd been instructed to watch over me. Why would Lord Toric order such a thing?

My stomach in a knot over my failure to speak up to Lord Toric and Akantha's harassment, I left my plate where it was, poured a tumbler of water, and walked toward one of the unoccupied curtained areas. I wasn't hungry—I'd only been willing to go back to the buffet table because Lord Toric wanted to—and now that the alien Lord was gone, I no longer felt compelled to try to keep up an act to win favor. I was the only Obligate who'd had any direct contact with Lord Toric, and

I figured I'd either made a good impression that would help me in the rankings, or I'd screwed up and there was nothing I could do about it now. I wasn't like Kalindi or Meribel. I had no talents with which to entertain a crowd. I wasn't even really sure how or if pleasing the other Calistans in attendance would affect the ranks of favor, and at the moment I didn't really care.

Confusion fluttered through my stomach as I sat on a padded bench with my cup. I was still angry at myself for letting an opportunity to express my opinions to Lord Toric slip away. But I was much more irritated because of something I didn't really want to admit . . . I truly enjoyed the alien Lord's presence.

He was intimidating, but as I'd felt in the throne room the first time I'd seen him, he possessed a depth that piqued my curiosity. And I couldn't say how I knew it, but there was also profound pain—anguish, even—lurking behind his gaze. In spite of my feelings about the Tournament, I couldn't help wanting to understand how someone like Lord Toric had come to know such pain.

Those things aside, he was so powerfully, magnetically handsome it was all I could do to keep from fidgeting like a silly girl when I was sitting next to him. I tried to tell myself it was ridiculous to be attracted to the very man who was responsible for taking me from Mother and Lana and stealing my future from me, but . . . I couldn't seem to help my reaction to him. And I couldn't help feeling that as long as he was nearby I was safe from harm, and *that* was probably the most ridiculous of all the thoughts spinning through my mind.

I let out an exasperated sigh.

What was wrong with me? I had come to the ballroom determined to give Lord Toric a piece of my mind, and I was hiding away and mooning over the way my heart bumped every time he turned his blue-green gaze on me. I hadn't even managed to try to follow Iris's advice about expressing a desire to serve him.

"Maya."

I looked up. Four Obligates stood in a row peering at me—Kalindi, Meribel, Cheytan, and Riki.

I shifted on my seat. Despite their smiles, something told me they didn't intend to be friendly. Where was Britta? She was the only one I might consider an ally, but if she'd continued the pace of drinking I'd seen earlier, she was probably passed out somewhere by now.

Not wanting them to come and stand over me, trapping me in between the two gauzy curtains, I stood and walked forward. "Enjoying the party?"

Kalindi brushed ahead of the others, came to me, and took my cup. She set it on a small table and then took both my hands in hers. She pulled me back and practically forced me down to sit on the bench next to her. She leaned in with a conspiratorial smile. The other women crowded in. I stifled a sigh.

"You're the only one who got to talk to him," Kalindi said, her eyes bright as a bird with a sparkly object in its sights. "What was he like?"

"What did he say?" Meribel asked.

Cheytan and Riki asked questions, too, right on top of each other.

I pulled my hands away from Kalindi's and angled my knees toward her, giving me an excuse to scoot back a little.

"He was very gentlemanly," I said.

"What else?" Kalindi leaned forward and put her hand on my wrist, tugging at me a little.

"We didn't have much time to converse," I said. "We were listening to the music."

Meribel gave me a sharp look that glinted with jealousy. "And then he had to *leave*. Why did he take off so fast?"

I shrugged. "He didn't say. Some urgent business."

"It's not fair," Riki said, not bothering to hide her irritation.

I shrank back a little. "It was out of my control."

All of them were examining me, looking over my hair, my clothes.

"Maya, I see the desserts have been brought out," a male voice called from the entrance of my section. "Would you like to sample them?"

I looked past the women to see Orion standing behind them. He gave me a half-smile, and I let out a relieved breath.

"That sounds lovely, Orion." I stood up and turned sideways so I could move between Riki and Cheytan. I took his offered arm and then looked over my shoulder at the women. "You're all welcome to join us."

I didn't wait to see if they followed.

"Thank you," I whispered to Orion. "Are you done serving your nobleman?"

"Yes, he decided to retire for the night. That guard is watching you." He tipped his head in a subtle movement toward the Calistan who had stayed behind when Lord Toric left.

"I know, but I'm not sure why," I said.

"How was your time with Lord Toric?" Orion asked, his eyes still on the guard.

I gave a little laugh. "I don't know. I may have made a fool of myself. But if I did, he was quite kind."

"The two of you make a striking pair."

I glanced up to see if he was teasing me, but he looked sincere. I wasn't sure how to respond.

At the dessert table, I placed a delicate little square cake on a napkin. The aromas of lemon and vanilla wafted to my nose. I took a bite and couldn't help a hum of enjoyment.

"The other women certainly didn't appreciate that he spent his limited time here with me," I said, my lips pulling to one side in a frown. I took another bite of the delicious little cake.

"Of course they're jealous," Orion said. He arched a brow at me. "Regardless of the standings, I think it's clear to everyone that Lord Toric has a personal preference for you."

I stopped chewing for a second. Then I swallowed and looked at him out of the corners of my eyes. "It was just luck that I was the only Obligate he spoke with this evening. A messenger arrived and he had to leave."

"It's not just that you were the only one he spoke to. He truly favors you," Orion said, then bumped my arm with his elbow. "Just trust me on this, would you?"

"It's not that I don't trust you . . ." I shook my head. Perhaps Lord Toric *had* given me small acknowledgements during the ceremonies in the throne room, but Orion was implying something much more overt. "I'm not being coy. He may be a bit intrigued by me, but beyond that I don't think you're right."

"Oh, I'm right."

"Well, in any case, I hope my interaction with him helped me in some way. How did your evening with the nobleman go?" I asked, eager to shift the conversation to something other than me.

"I could have done better, but I think it went as well as possible considering that I have not been trained for this. When Lord Toric reviews the evening, I can only hope he sees that I'm doing my best and that I am eager to improve."

"When he reviews the evening? What do you mean?"

"We're being recorded. Nearly all the time, aside from when we're in our private rooms."

"What?" I gave him a wide-eyed look of horror.

"How do you think they were able to rate us during the first challenge?"

My cheeks heated with embarrassment. Of course we were under surveillance, how stupid of me not to realize it.

"Don't worry, he'll see the way those women descended on you," Orion assured me.

I giggled ruefully. "Thanks again for getting me out of there."

His face turned serious, his brows drawn low. "We must be very careful, Maya. I'm starting to think that there are more perils here than we want to see."

Before I could probe his comment with a question, I felt someone at my elbow and turned. It was the guard.

"I've been instructed to escort you back to your quarters," he said to me.

I glanced around and realized that the party was dispersing. But none of the other Obligates seemed to have a private escort. They were gathering near the doorway under Akantha's watchful eye. I looked up at the guard in question and then glanced at Orion.

"Must she go with you?" Orion asked. "Why can't she go with the rest of us?"

"On Lord Toric's order," the guard said.

"It's okay," I said. I didn't want Orion to get in trouble. "This guard came in with Lord Toric, and I'm sure there's no reason to distrust him."

I gave the guard a tight smile, but his stony expression remained the same.

"Come with me," he said, and turned on his heel with military precision.

I gave Orion a little wave and followed the guard. As we passed the Obligates, I could feel their curious stares.

Akantha stepped forward, blocking our way. "The Offered

come with me," she said. She was nearly as tall as the muscular guard.

"I'm escorting this Earthen on the order of Lord Toric," he said. "Move aside."

I nearly smiled with satisfaction. But the look she shot me wiped away any urge to gloat openly.

After a moment, she stepped back. With her hands on her hips, she looked down her nose at me as I passed.

I swallowed hard. I had a feeling she would find a way to punish me for this special treatment later, though I couldn't understand why she would care so deeply whether I walked with this guard or with the rest of the Obligates back to my quarters.

The guard and I drew many stares as we walked through the hallways of the palace. When we finally reached my quarters, I felt nearly weak with relief.

"Keep the door locked," the guard said gruffly. His dark brown face was etched in stone, but I thought I saw a hint of kindness in his pale gray eyes. "Don't open it for anyone but your Tournament guide."

"Thank you for escorting me." For a moment I wondered if I should curtsy. After all, he was Calistan and I was Earthen. But he was a guard, not a nobleman or royalty, so I just gave him a nod.

I was hoping Iris would be waiting for me. She hadn't been at the party—none of the guides had—but I wished to tell her about the evening, ask her opinion on my conversation with

Lord Toric, and see if she knew anything about why he was called away.

I was exhausted but not yet ready to sleep. I sat on my bed, looking around the small room and suddenly feeling extremely alone. I bent down and removed my shoes from my throbbing feet.

I had no idea what was coming next. We hadn't been told when the next challenge of the Tournament would begin, or whether we would have to gather in the throne room again to review our ranks of favor, or . . . anything. I felt like a puppet in a show, a game piece getting scooted around a board.

My mind swam and my heart ached. In the span of a couple of days, I had lost everything I knew of my life and passed through a portal to a strange land. I'd fought death, watched others die, and then dressed up like a princess and listened to music with an alien Lord.

The alien Lord Toric . . .

Curling up on my side, I drew my knees to my chest. In addition to my swimming mind and aching heart, my stomach fluttered whenever I remembered Lord Toric's eyes boring into me. He looked at me as if he saw more than just my face, my hair, and my dress.

Or maybe I was just imagining things? Perhaps I only wanted to believe he favored me because I wanted so badly to survive? Any maybe I wanted more than just survival . . . there was something about *him* I wanted.

I pressed my hand into my stomach, my mouth suddenly

dry.

Something was happening, something had been set in motion. I could not describe it and did not understand it, but I knew it all the same.

I closed my eyes and drifted on this new swirl of emotions and fears and uncertainties . . .

"Maya."

I opened my eyes, disoriented. I'd fallen asleep in my clothes with the lamp still lit.

I sat up and my heart hammered in alarm. A man stood near the door, his face in shadow. I gasped. For a moment I thought it might be Lord Toric but then he stepped forward.

"Sir Jeric?" I swung my feet to the floor, suddenly glad that I hadn't changed out of my clothes.

But what was he doing here? I thought of the guard's warning, and my eyes flicked to the door.

"I did not mean to alarm you." He held one hand out, palm down, as if to try to soothe me. "But what I told you before, about communicating with your sister—"

"You can take me to speak to Lana?" My heart was beating almost painfully from surprise at Jeric's presence in my room and the prospect of talking to my twin.

"Yes." He took two long strides toward me, and his gaze bore down like a weight. "But if you ever tell anyone that I offered you this opportunity, if you invoke my name in any way, it will mean death for you and exile for me. I want to do this for you, but this is strictly forbidden by the word of the sacred texts."

I nodded, though trepidation pinged through me. "I promise I will not tell."

"No matter what?"

"No matter what." I swallowed hard. My intuition was sending out little warnings, but I shoved them away. I could not turn down a chance to speak to my sister, and I didn't care that it was forbidden by the Calistans' sacred texts. After all, it was not my religion.

"There is a man, a servant, who will be waiting outside. After I leave, wait for a count of ten and then open the door. He will take you to speak with your Lana."

Taking a deep breath to try to calm my speeding pulse, I managed a smile. "Thank you, Sir Jeric. You have no idea how much this means to me. Thank you for this kindness."

When I said "kindness," his lips twitched in a tiny smile, but his eyes darkened.

He turned to leave, and I took a step and stretched out my hand. "Wait. Why are you doing this for me?"

He stopped at the door and his face softened. For a moment his eyes reminded me of Lord Toric's. But then his eyes hardened and any warmth that may have been there disappeared. "Because I may need you to do something for me. This is my first demonstration that I can give you the things you desire. And I can keep doing so if you are willing help me in turn."

And then he was through the door and gone before I could

press him further.

Something important for the brother of the Lord? What could I possibly offer?

With shaking hands I pulled on the flat shoes that I'd worn from Earthenfell while I counted slowly to ten. When I opened the door, a Calistan man was there. He was dressed more like a guard than a servant—in ankle-high boots, gray trousers, and a white military-cut jacket.

He handed me a strange bonnet-style hat with a deep brim. "Put this on and keep your head down. You must hide your face as much as possible."

I slipped it over my head and tied it under my chin. Then he held out a plain navy trench coat. I pushed my arms into the sleeves and secured the three large buttons in front.

"Keep quiet," he said, and then he was off at a swift pace.

I nearly had to run to keep up with his much longer legs. We took many turns, a winding route through what appeared to be little-used minor hallways, and climbed staircases. Twice we got into elevators that shot us upward at stomach-dropping speed. The few times we passed anyone I dared not look up, and the man leading me never hesitated or slowed.

Finally, he stopped and I peeked left and right. We had reached the end of a silent corridor.

"Go up that staircase." He pointed to a narrow set of stairs that wound out of sight in a tight spiral. "At the top, go through the door and wait."

I stared at him a moment, hoping for more information.

But he just stared back, obviously waiting for me to depart.

I nodded and began climbing the stairs. Every six steps or so, there was a tiny light built into the wall, and those were the only illumination in the windowless staircase. The ceiling was low and claustrophobic, and I had the sensation of being very high up. Perhaps even in one of the pointed spires that I'd seen from the ground when I'd first arrived on Calisto.

My leg muscles burning from the long climb, I stopped abruptly when I realized the staircase ended in a few more steps, at a door. I turned the handle and it swung inward. On the other side was an empty round room with two high windows a couple of feet above my head.

I pulled off my hat, dropped it, and turned a slow circle. How was I supposed to communicate with Lana?

My chest tightened as I began to wonder if it had been a trick. No one except Jeric and the man who'd guided me even knew where I was.

I ran to the door but too late realized there was no handle on my side. Sliding my fingers along its smooth surface, I searched for a way to open it.

With panic rising through me, I spun to search the room itself. It was growing brighter, but not from light coming through the windows. A bright pulsing ball the size of my fist hung in the middle of the room.

I pressed back against the door as the light brightened and swelled to the size of my head. It grew too bright to watch, and I slid to the floor and hid my eyes behind my arms.

Too scared to cry out, I huddled against the door.

Then the painful flare subsided. I cracked one eyelid open to find a ring of light hanging in the air. But it wasn't just a ring of light. It was like looking through a window. There were trees, a bird flitted by, and . . .

I scrambled to my feet. "Lana!"

My sister was there, sitting at the base of a tree with her skeins of colored thread. She was still piling up the colorful bundles as if she'd just arrived in the orchard at the start of the work day.

Her hands froze and she raised her head at the sound of her name. Then her hands began to tremble and her head whipped left and right. "M—Maya?" she whispered. "Is that you?"

I ran toward the ring of light. "Yes, it's me! I can see you. I'm looking at you through a portal. I—I don't know how, but—" My voice faltered and I blinked back tears. "Oh Lana, I miss you so terribly."

"Are you okay? How are you able to do this?" She rose to her knees but didn't stand.

"Yes, I'm fine," I said, brushing tears from my cheeks. "Sir Jer—I mean, someone offered to let me talk to you, and of course I jumped at the chance. How are you? How is Mother? Is Rand collecting for you?"

"Rand and a few others helped with my collections yesterday and are helping today too. Court even said he would pitch in. Maybe he truly does feel bad about what he did to you. Mother is . . . she's devastated, of course." Lana shook her head. "I just can't believe I'm talking to you right now."

My mind reeled as images and faces from home rushed through my thoughts. It felt like I'd been gone for years, but this was probably only Lana's second day back at work after the Selection and Departure ceremonies.

"I know, I can't believe it either." I lifted one hand, wishing I could reach through the portal to touch Lana's arm, to dig my fingers in the brown earth.

I sucked in a breath. The window was shrinking. "I think it's disappearing." I said. "Wait, not yet! Lana!"

I stumbled backward as the border of the portal contracted and formed a white ball of light that finally forced me to squeeze my eyes closed.

I turned at the sound of the door opening. Blinking rapidly, I tried to see who it was, but I was blinded by the blotches dotting my vision.

Rough hands slammed some sort of cover over my head. I struggled, lashing out and clawing at the arms that held me.

Then something hit the side of my head with such force that the crack against my skull was the last thing I registered before everything slipped away.

I FELT MY body moving, but it wasn't under my power. Hands were under my arms and grasping my legs. Then I was lying on a mat or perhaps on the floor. My nerves seemed partially numbed, my senses only somewhat useful in telling me what was happening, and my muscles completely slack.

There were voices, but my brain was too slow to try to pick out more than a word or two here and there.

Lana.

I remembered seeing my sister through the portal.

I should have tried to climb through the ring of light. Even if I burned up in the blue-white glow, it would have been worth trying.

Hands rolled me onto one side, and then there was a sharp zing at the back of my neck.

Darkness crowded in and numbed me from the world.

16

Toric

WHEN VICTOR WOKE me to inform me that Akantha needed to speak to me urgently, I couldn't imagine what the emergency might be. I pulled on clothes and went to my receiving room, where the Mistress of Tournament had come to inform me that Maya was missing. My first thought was that Calvin had failed, that he and Maya had been attacked.

But as I pushed the fog of sleep from my brain, I realized that didn't make sense. Calvin had escorted Maya to her room just as I'd asked. At least five hours had passed since he'd reported back to me after leaving her safely. He did not know that since giving that order I'd decided she needed constant guard, so he'd left her in her locked room, and another guard had arrived later to stay outside her door.

I took a deep breath in through my nose to try sharpen my

mind, to catch up.

Maya. She was in danger.

"How could she be missing?" I was unable to keep emotion from my voice.

The Mistress of Tournament lifted a shoulder. She was trying to make me believe that the entire situation bored her, but I saw the dark spark of pleasure in her eyes. "Her room is empty."

There were a few minutes, maybe even half an hour, between when Calvin had left her and the new guard, Dorn, had arrived. I had not instructed Dorn to check on Maya, as I assumed she would be asleep. In any case I preferred not to alert her to the fact that she was under watch. But in that short time, someone had taken her.

I gave Akantha a hard, narrow-eyed stare and barreled toward her. "You seem none too concerned." Her eyes popped wide, and she backed up to the wall. I towered over her, seething. "Did you have something to do with her disappearance? Is there something you're not telling me, Akantha?"

She shook her head vehemently. "No, my Lord. Of course not."

I wasn't sure I believed her.

Pushing past her, I went to the door.

"Alert the Master of the Guard," I said to the two men posted just inside. "One of the Offered has been abducted from her room. Her name is Maya, and she must not be harmed."

The guards didn't completely mask their surprise at the

level of concern I was showing for an Earthen woman who wasn't even part of my harem. I was too frantic to care.

"Maybe she simply tried to run away." Akantha's smug voice made my blood run hot with rage.

I whirled around. "Get out, if you have nothing useful to offer. *Get out!*" I stormed at her.

She ducked her head and scurried away.

My pulse was pounding in my temples as my fury at Akantha and dread over Maya's fate mingled, sending adrenaline surging through me.

Calvin arrived, standing between me and the open chamber door. He was touching his earpiece, likely calling for a second guard. Quick heavy footsteps approached and Dorn arrived, his face ashen.

Dorn was only a year or two into his service, one of the youngest of the elite royal guards. He fell to one knee at my feet. "My Lord, I never left her door and never let anyone in, I swear." His voice shook, and I knew he feared he would lose his job or maybe even face imprisonment.

"I know," I said. "She was taken before you took your post. You may rise."

I turned to Calvin and beckoned to him. I did not want to reveal Maya's importance to me, but I wasn't sure what else to do. The Priestess had all but declared that one of the Offered women was vital to our path back to Earthenfell, and I knew that woman was Maya. My feelings for her aside, Maya's safety was important in a much greater sense.

"This is in the strictest confidence," I said to Calvin. "I need you to accompany me on a sweep of the palace. I can . . . sense Maya's energy if I am in close enough proximity to her. But it must be only us. I need you to send Dorn away."

"My Lord, it would be a violation to my duty to allow you to walk the palace with only one guard. I believe that Palovich is trustworthy."

I clenched my jaw for a moment. Calvin would insist on protocol, and I couldn't blame him for it—he was doing his job. I nodded. "Call for Palovich. Tell Dorn he's dismissed. And tell Palovich to catch up with us. I don't want to wait."

Calvin went to Dorn, and I ducked into my dressing room and shoved on some shoes. Calvin accompanied me out the door.

I turned left, intending to head away from the hallways with the royal apartments. I believed either Jeric or Akantha or both were behind Maya's abduction, and if I were right, the royal quarters were the last place they'd keep her. There were too many servants passing in and out, and someone would have spotted her.

At an elevator, I paused. Up or down? Some of the towers were little used, and they were only a couple of floors up from our location. We'd go up first.

Palovich caught up just as Calvin and I stepped onto the elevator. We rode up as far as it would take us. There were three towers on our side of the palace. I headed toward the closest one, and my guards followed me up the narrow, winding staircase. The room at the top held only some dusty furniture.

The next tower housed a mechanical room, a communication relay tower. No Maya.

I wasn't surprised that I didn't find her in either of the first two towers. I would have felt her energy. If she were alive, anyway. But that's why I had to check with my own eyes and not just rely on sensing her.

I wasn't sure what I would do if I found her lifeless body.

At the top of the stairs of the third tower there was a woman's hat on the landing, a big floppy fabric thing.

My pulse tripped. I clutched the hat and pushed open the door to the tower room. It was empty. But I had the distinct feeling she'd been there. It wasn't that I could sense any of her energy, but . . . the discarded hat was so out of place it piqued my suspicion.

"Let's try the basement," I said, going on instinct.

It took nearly twenty minutes to take a series of three elevators and several staircases to the bowels of the palace.

The air somehow felt heavier in the basement, as if the weight of the enormous palace and all the people above pressed down over us.

I hesitated, unsure which way to turn. And then there was a flicker, like a little shock of electricity that circled my heart. It was faint, but I recognized it immediately.

I angled to the right, jogged to the next intersection, and then took a sharp left turn. The basement was a series of warehouses, staging spaces for ceremonial items, and storage for food, furniture, raw materials, vehicles, and all manner of other items.

Calvin and Palovich had illuminated their flashlights, and they swung the beams back and forth.

I could feel Maya, and her energy was growing stronger. I sped up to a run, having to backtrack a couple of times when I made a wrong turn and felt her energy weaken.

Calvin and Palovich followed me silently, breathing almost as heavily as I was. I led them into a dim storage room full of wheeled laundry bins. There were rows of shelves holding stacks of folded clothing and linens.

Maya's energy pulsed, calling to me like a heartbeat through the room.

I ran to the shelves. All I saw were stacks of fabric, but I knew she was there.

I peered down. Yes, she was very close.

I pulled stacks of sheets from the lowest shelf, digging into them and pushing them aside. There was a small hand, an arm. I cleared away more linens, and Calvin knelt next to me to help. Palovich shone his flashlight over our shoulders, and the light glanced off Maya's pale face.

She'd been laid out behind the stacks of linens, completely concealed in the middle of the shelf in the dark storage room. If not for my ability to sense her energy, she probably never would have been found.

"Maya," I breathed, reaching for her arm and pulling her toward me. I hovered over her and let out a gasp of relief when

I felt her faint breath against my cheek. She was alive.

Her limbs were limp, and her hair was tangled across her forehead. I lifted her in my arms, pulling her to my chest. She felt as light and fragile as a bird. Why she had been concealed here, and what her abductor had planned to do next, I couldn't guess.

"Should I call for a medic?" Calvin asked.

"I want my personal doctor called to my chambers immediately," I said. I couldn't take my eyes off Maya's face. "The Priestess, too. And no one else."

On the way back to my chambers, the palace around me seemed to blur to the background as my entire focus was absorbed by the feel of Maya's slight weight in my arms, her side pressed against my chest, and her beautiful, too-still face.

The Priestess and my doctor waited in the receiving room of my chambers, both rising as I entered. I hurried past them to my sleeping chamber and gently lowered Maya to the bed.

I glanced at Dr. Liev, an older man who had been my family's physician since I was born. "She's breathing, but she hasn't stirred since we found her."

He nodded and quickly pulled a diagnostic cuff from his satchel and wrapped it around Maya's wrist. Readouts began pinging on his handheld monitor, and I watched his face anxiously for any clue about her condition.

"Her vitals are in the acceptable range. Except for her brainwaves, which is to be expected for an unconscious patient." Dr. Liev looked up at me and then back down at the readouts. "She suffered a bump to the head, but that is not the only cause of her cataleptic state. It appears she was drugged, but the drug used is unknown."

"What could that mean?"

He shook his head. "I'm not sure. And because the drug is unknown I can't prescribe an antidote. She seems stable for now. She should be kept warm and undisturbed, and if she has not regained consciousness within two hours, she should receive fluids to prevent dehydration."

I pulled the edge of the bed cover up and folded it over her. She looked like a doll nestled in my huge bed.

"I will leave the cuff on her so that I'll be immediately alerted of any change," Dr. Liev continued. "I'll return to check on her within two hours. Sooner if her condition changes."

I waited for Dr. Liev to depart and then turned to the Priestess. "She is the one, I'm sure of it. The Earthen woman you spoke of, the one in the new volume of the sacred texts. Could someone else know, too?"

The Priestess was staring down at Maya so intently, and for a moment I wasn't sure if the Priestess had heard me. Then she turned to me, but her eyes roamed around me as if she saw something in the air that was visible only to her. "You may be right," she finally said. "And although we have no proof, it is probably not coincidence that someone singled her out."

"Who would want to harm her?" I peered at her, trying to discern whether she suspected anyone.

"That I do not know, my Lord. But you must be vigilant

and assume that anyone could be an enemy." She finally turned her gaze on me. "You suspect someone already?"

"I have a couple of guesses about who my enemies might be," I said. My fingers curled and tightened against my palms. "Can you help me discover whether my brother and Akantha were involved?"

She hesitated for only a second and then nodded firmly. "I will use all the resources at my disposal to investigate."

"We have another problem," I said, my stomach knotting with dread. "The next challenge in the Tournament begins in less than a day. What if she has not awakened by then or is too weak to compete?"

The Priestess drew a deep breath. "Missing a challenge will put her too far out of the running to earn enough rank to emerge the winner," she said heavily.

We both looked down at Maya's still form. I willed her to stir, prayed for her eyes to open. But not even the tiniest twitch of movement passed over her tranquil face.

After the Priestess left, wanting to begin her investigation into Maya's abduction, I pulled a chair over to the side of the bed and sat with my forearms resting on my knees and my gaze trained on Maya. After some time, I could resist no longer. I shifted the covers to find her hand, and I held it gently in mine for a long moment before placing it on her stomach and covering her again. I brushed a few strands of hair off her forehead. Her skin was too cold, her limb too limp.

I heard the soft complaint of ancient door hinges and

turned to see Victor standing just inside the chamber. "My Lord, may I get anything for you? A light meal, perhaps?"

Had he seen me touch Maya's hair? His energy was calm, and his curiosity did not seem piqued. Either he hadn't seen, or his professional detachment prevented him from any reaction, even a well-concealed one.

"I have no appetite at the moment," I said.

Victor inclined his head and slipped out. With my elbows propped on my knees, I dropped my face to my hands.

Bit by bit, I was revealing my feelings for Maya. Since she'd arrived on Calisto, I'd been unable to stay away from her and unable to completely mask how deeply I was drawn to her. Even though I'd had every intention of treating her the same as the other Offered and keeping my attraction to her secret, I couldn't help feeling that my weakness and failure had somehow led to her current peril.

A soft sound, barely more than a sigh, drew my attention back to Maya. Was it her or just my imagination?

Not daring to breathe, I watched her. Her eyelids twitched. Her breathing seemed to have deepened a bit. I leaned closer to her.

"Maya?" I said softly. "Can you hear me?"

Her eyelids opened, and her blue eyes stared upward. For a second the look in her eyes was so vacant and unseeing, my heart lurched in panic.

But then she swallowed and turned her head just enough to look at me.

"Lord Toric," she said, her words barely more than a croak. "It was you. You came for me."

I let out a long, shaking breath and gave her a wavering smile. "Yes, I found you."

I didn't want to move from her side, but I knew she needed water. "Stay still. I'm going to pour you a glass."

My heart soared and my hands trembled as I poured water into a crystal tumbler. I set the glass next to the bed so I could tuck another pillow behind her head. Her dark hair brushed my arm, sending invisible sparks dancing along my skin.

I tipped the glass to her lips and she took a few sips.

She cleared her throat and gave me a bashful look from under her eyelashes. "Thank you. I bet I am the first Earthen to be waited on by the Guardian Lord of Calisto and Earth in such a manner."

I didn't try to hide my amusement, or the emotion that was welling up through me like a tidal wave.

It was as if a layer of an invisible barrier between us had fallen away. I did not understand exactly what it meant but knew from the depths of my heart and soul that a meaningful shift had taken place. And somehow, I knew that she knew it, too.

She held my gaze as I reached out and swept a strand of hair from her cheek.

At the sound of the door opening behind me, my hand flinched back and I rose to my feet. It was Dr. Liev.

"I see our patient is awake," the doctor said in the kindly

voice that had soothed me when I was a child.

He set his satchel on my chair and flipped through Maya's diagnostic readouts on his handheld device. "How are you feeling, young woman?" He glanced up at her.

"Weak, and my head is pounding. But glad to be alive and awake," she said. Her voice already sounded a bit stronger.

Now that she seemed to be out of the worst of the danger, some of my former anger was returning. I could not question Maya in front of the doctor, but I needed to know what she remembered. I needed to know who had done this to her.

"May I speak to you, my Lord?" the doctor said.

We moved to the balcony, and I positioned myself so that Maya was still in my line of sight.

"She needs rest, food, and fluids," the doctor said. "I will give her something for her head. As far as I can tell, there is no serious injury."

"And the Tournament?" I asked. I did not want her to compete. I wanted more than anything to keep her with me, out of harm's way.

"What is the next challenge?"

"The game of survival, to begin tomorrow morning." My stomach curled into a hard knot at the thought of it. The game of survival was less brutal than the first culling challenge, but just as perilous. As its nickname indicated, it was not just straight survival challenge, but one of strategy as well.

Dr. Liev's face grew grave. "I doubt she will be in any sort of shape to face that type of challenge."

He looked at me, likely thinking the same thing I was: What other choice was there for Maya, except to compete regardless of her condition?

"Can you give her anything? Something to strengthen her?" I asked.

"I will give her a healing infusion, but it will only do so much. Ideally, she would take a week or more to rest and build her strength back. Shall I have her transferred to the servants' clinic?"

"No, administer the treatment here," I said quickly. I cleared my throat, regretting that I'd spoken too hastily. My mind spun as I tried to think of a way to recover. "She's only just regained consciousness, and I think it best if she doesn't have to move. Don't you agree?"

A flicker of a question passed over his face. "As you wish, my Lord."

I could only imagine what was running through his mind, how my protectiveness over Maya appeared from his perspective. But I simply couldn't let her out of my sight, regardless of how questionable my behavior might seem.

He gave her a transdermal mist injection, strict instructions to get up only for essential needs for the next eight hours, and then departed.

I knew I needed to call for the Priestess again so that we could discuss how to proceed, knowing Maya was awake. Not that I imagined we had many options. But more than that, I wanted to extend my time alone with Maya, even if only for a few minutes.

"Are you hungry?" I asked. "I can order anything you want. It would be good for you to eat something, to help get your strength back."

"Thank you, my Lord. I don't think I'm quite ready for food." Maya's cheeks colored. "My Lord, I need to use—um . . ."

I tilted my head, waiting for her to finish, and then it struck me that she was trying to tell me she needed to use the restroom. "Oh! Of course. I can call for a female servant to help you."

"I don't, um, think I need that *much* assistance, thank you." Her cheeks burned deeper pink, but she raised her chin. "Perhaps just assistance getting up? I'm sorry, Lord Toric, I do not know the proper protocol." She looked down at her hands.

I chuckled. "I'm not sure there *is* a protocol for our current situation. We will just have to make it up as we go."

She looked at me out of the corners of her eyes, and when her mouth widened just a little in a small, grateful smile, it made my heart sing.

She pushed the covers down to her waist, and I realized she was still dressed in the lovely pale green gown she'd worn to the ballroom. It was wrinkled and smudged with dust now, and when she sat up and swung her legs over the edge of the bed, I caught sight of a torn hem edge.

When her feet touched the floor and she shifted her weight off the bed, her knees buckled. I took a lunging step forward, bending to catch her before she fell. Her forehead brushed my chin, and she clutched at my forearms.

"I'm sorry, I did not guess I would be quite this weak. I—oh!" She gasped as I swept her up in my arms and carried her toward my dressing room and bathroom.

I looked down at her. Surely she could feel my heart racing. "You should save your strength."

She swallowed, her eyes wide with apprehension. After a moment she relaxed a little. "Thank you. You're much too kind and accommodating, my Lord. I'm embarrassed to be such a nuisance."

"You're not a nuisance in any way. You're a resident in my palace, and as such I'm to blame for your mistreatment and abduction." I was fully aware that my words might sound hypocritical to her ears. After all, Maya had watched some of her comrades die in the first challenge of the Tournament. The Earthen Offered were not *exactly* guests here. But what had happened to Maya was certainly not part of the Tournament. "And I want to know who is responsible for what happened to you. When you are settled back in bed, I hope you'll tell me every detail you remember."

She glanced at me and seemed to hesitate but then shook her head. "I didn't see anything. Whoever it was snuck up on me and put a bag over my head."

I ground my teeth and tried to hide my disappointment. I was hoping she'd be able to accuse Jeric outright. I set her on her feet just inside the doorway of the large marble bathroom. She grasped the doorjamb with one hand but seemed steady enough to stand.

"Perhaps together we can discover some detail that will help us identify your abductor," I said. "I will leave a robe for you to change into right out here." I pointed to a bench in the dressing room that adjoined the bathroom. "You'll be okay?"

She nodded, and her cheeks flushed again. "Yes, I think so. Thank you, my Lord." She disappeared behind the closed door of the bathroom.

I found a pale blue silk robe with a soft cotton lining, laid it on the bench, and then exited the dressing room and shut the door behind me to give her some privacy.

I paced outside the door, my stomach tight and my pulse thin and fast, pausing only long enough to go ask Victor to send for the Priestess.

I wondered if Maya had any idea of the effect she had on me. How badly I wanted to call off the Tournament, abandon all traditions outlined by the sacred texts, and keep her here in my chambers where I knew she was safe.

And what if Maya really remembered nothing of who abducted her? How would I prove that Jeric was involved? I was torn between wanting to storm through the palace in search of my treacherous brother and staying by Maya's side.

When she emerged from the dressing room wearing the robe I'd provided, she gave me a hesitant smile. "My favorite dress back home was exactly this color," she said, looking down at the robe.

"It suits you perfectly." I forced myself not to stare and

instead offered my arm. "Do you think you can walk to the bed chamber?" I almost hoped she couldn't. Though of course I wanted her strength to return, I enjoyed the feel of her in my arms.

She nodded but still took my arm. "A little movement before I rest again might be a good thing. And I truly do not want to impose any more than I have. I understand if you'd like me to go back to my room."

"I can certainly arrange that, but why don't you stay here a bit longer so we can talk about what happened leading up to your abduction?"

"My Lord." I turned to see Victor standing inside the bedroom chamber door. "The Priestess has come."

"Send her in," I said and then returned my attention to Maya and helping her back into bed.

The Priestess strode in, her robes flowing behind her. Her slight breathlessness was the only crack in her composure. The Priestess looked over at Maya and then slowly angled her body away from me and toward the bed.

"You are Maya," the Priestess said, her voice quiet but solemn, as if she were making a ceremonial pronouncement.

17

Maya

SINCE I'D AWAKENED in Lord Toric's chambers, part of me suspected that I had never actually woken up at all, and my mind had spun me into a strange, vivid dream. How could I possibly be resting in the alien Lord's bed while he fetched water for me, carried me to the bathroom, and hovered over me like a worried mother hen?

It all seemed unreal. And yet, there was *something*, an unspoken zip of energy between us that made this unexpected situation feel less outlandish than it should have. It made no sense, but maybe I could blame it on the knock to the head I'd suffered.

When the Priestess came in, I felt my face flush out of embarrassment that I couldn't curtsy. "I apologize for my condition and my inability to greet you properly," I said. "I mean no disrespect."

"You are forgiven, of course," the Priestess said. She glanced at Lord Toric. "Do we know who is responsible?"

"She says her abductor did not reveal himself. Or herself," Lord Toric said.

They both turned to me. "Could you tell us exactly what happened, from the beginning?" the Priestess asked.

I shifted under the covers. I'd been dreading this since I woke up. How could I explain without revealing that Jeric had allowed me to communicate with Lana? I did not believe he was responsible for what happened afterward—it made no sense that he would allow me to speak with my sister only to then abduct and drug me. And he'd made it very clear that if I told anyone what he'd allowed me to do, we'd both suffer extremely grave consequences.

"I had fallen asleep in my room," I said. "I woke to a bag pulled over my head and a hard bump to my head followed by a pinch at the back of my neck. A shot or a shock, I'm not sure which, but immediately after I passed out." I tensed, half-expecting that my implant would somehow alert them to my half-truths.

"And the light was still on?" she asked.

I nodded. "Yes, but the bag was slipped over my head before I fully woke up, so I didn't see who was in my room."

"Did it sound like one person? More than one?" Lord Toric asked.

"Possibly two, but it happened so fast I can't be sure."

"Did you hear anything that might indicate your abductor was male or female? Even just a grunt?" he asked.

"I'm sorry, I don't recall anything like that."

He and the Priestess exchanged a glance. I wondered what interest the Priestess could have in my situation—it seemed more a concern for the palace guard or even the Mistress of Tournament than the highest-ranking religious leader of Calisto—but it wasn't my place to demand an explanation.

"If you remember any other details, report them right away," the Priestess said and then beckoned to Lord Toric. The two of them moved to the balcony to converse in private.

Did they see through my fabrication about where my abduction had taken place? It felt terrible to lie, but I didn't want to cause trouble for Sir Jeric after he'd done something so risky for me. And I didn't want to get in trouble, either. It wasn't my fault that someone had taken me against my will. If that hadn't happened, I would have returned to my room and fallen asleep and no one would have been the wiser about Lana and the portal in the tower.

I looked around the bed chamber, feeling free to stare a little while no one was watching. It was a rounded room larger than my entire house on Earthenfell but contained few furnishings. A wide cabinet or wardrobe against one wall and a drink and food service stand near the balcony. Other than some plush, colorful rugs around the bed, there wasn't much to look at.

Was this where Lord Toric brought women from his

harem? Or was there a different bed chamber for such . . .
activities? I glanced at the pillows piled up at the head of the
large bed, and then over at the small bedside stand, which held
only a lamp and the glass of water Lord Toric had brought me.

After a few minutes, he and the Priestess came back in,
their heads bent together as they whispered. When they parted,
she went straight to the door without a backward glance.

Lord Toric returned to the chair he'd brought to the
bedside and scooted it close.

I shook my head and clasped my hands at my waist.
"I'm sorry I'm not more help," I said. "I wish I remembered
something."

He regarded me silently for a few seconds, and at first
I thought he was irritated that I wasn't more useful. But his
breathing had slowed, and his blue-green eyes were soft. He
wasn't irritated. He was concerned.

I pressed my lips into a faint smile. "You are not at all what
I expected." I sucked in a breath and my eyes widened. I hadn't
exactly meant to speak that thought aloud. "I mean—I don't
know what I mean. I'm sorry, I shouldn't have said that, my
Lord."

"No apology needed." He chuckled. "But I'm curious.
What did you expect?"

I clenched my hands together. "Someone far more . .
. stern, perhaps? You've been terribly kind to me, and to be
frank I find it—well, I find it difficult to reconcile."

"How so?"

I paused for a moment, my heart pounding as I considered what to say next. But since I'd already opened my mouth, I figured I might as well tell him what was on my mind.

"You take Earthens from their homes and bring them here to send some of them to their deaths. I did not expect such kindness from someone who subjects Earthens to such brutality," I said.

When his eyebrows rose and his face clouded, my heart lurched as my courage faltered. I'd overstepped. And now I'd have to face the consequence.

"You do not believe that the Tournament of the Offered is a fair payment for the protection of Earthens? For the very survival of your people?" he asked, his voice calm but chilly.

I took a breath and looked down at my hands, trying to summon back some courage. "I used to think it was fair, to be perfectly honest. Or maybe I just never really questioned it." I looked up at him. "Until I became one of those who might die."

A wave of great pain passed over his face, and he leaned forward and looked intently into my eyes. "You cannot die, Maya. I need you. I need you to win, to stay here with me." He spoke so softly for a moment I wasn't sure I'd heard correctly.

I could barely breathe. "My Lord?" I tilted my head in question, but I was hypnotized by his eyes, by the deep emotion etched on his face.

As if observing from outside my body, I watched as he gently covered my hands with one of his. The fingers of his other hand reached out slowly to trail across my cheek.

At his touch, I closed my eyes and a soft sigh escaped my lips. When I opened my eyes, my body was brimming with a heady rush of adrenaline. In spite of what I'd just said, I could not deny how deeply and intensely I was drawn to this man.

"I know I should not put this burden on you, but you must win," he said, his eyes turning passionately fierce. "You *must.*"

As if pulled by an invisible force, I leaned toward him just as he moved toward me. My breath stilled as our lips met, and it was as if every emotion I'd ever felt surged through me on a hot tidal wave that cleared my mind of every thought except the sensation of his Lord Toric's lips against mine.

Time stretched out as he pulled me deeper into the kiss. As in the moments just after I'd awakened with my implant, my senses seemed to explode. I could hear the movement of the breeze across the balcony, feel the vibrations of the soft yellow-taupe color of the walls, smell the subtle earthy scent that had been sprayed over Lord Toric's hair and skin. Sensations thrummed through my body, welling up like a storm building on the horizon.

When we parted I saw only his blue-green eyes.

Slowly, as if surfacing from deep water, I realized that a new truth had taken root inside me. He was right. I had to win the Tournament. With every fiber of my being, I knew that it was my destiny to become his. Even as I fiercely disagreed with his sacrifice of Earthens, I could not deny this truth.

The rush of emotion that had momentarily brought a

surge of energy now drained me of strength, and I leaned back against the pillows, trying to catch my breath.

Lord Toric kept a hold of my hand, and we gazed at each other in silence as seconds stretched out.

"I will find a way to win," I finally whispered.

He swallowed and blinked several times, as if coming out of a trance. "I'm sorry," he said. "I should not have said those things to you. I should not have kissed you."

"I don't regret either your words or your kiss," I said, suddenly feeling bold. My pulse was still racing.

He smiled faintly but let go of my hand. "I should not have done it, and I take responsibility." He drew a sharp breath and looked down. "I will try to delay the next challenge to give you more time to recover. It will be up to Akantha to agree to it, and she is not exactly my biggest supporter."

The next challenge. I'd forgotten it would come very soon. Tendrils of fear began twisting through me, reaching cold, rigid fingers through the heat of passion that Lord Toric's touch had lit up through my entire body.

"I will do what little I can for you," he said. "But I must warn you that I am forbidden from actually helping you to win the Tournament. For more reasons than you know, and reasons that I cannot speak of, you must win on your own."

I squinted, trying to read the subtext of what he was telling me. I knew to my very soul that he meant what he said—he wanted me to win—but I had the same prickling sense in the back of my mind that I'd felt when Iris had tried to hint to me about the fate of the Tournament losers. There was much more to all of this than I understood.

Somehow, I'd become part of something larger than I could imagine.

Movement near the door drew my attention. One of Lord Toric's Earthen servants stood just inside the chamber.

"My Lord," he said. His eyes flicked to me and then away. "The master of the guard wishes to speak to you."

Lord Toric stood. "I'll be there in fifteen minutes. Arrange for Maya to be transferred to her quarters under guard and to have a guard stationed at her door at all times. And send Calvin in."

The servant bowed and backed through the door.

Lord Toric turned to me. "I would have you stay here, but with servants constantly coming in and out, it is less secure than your locked room under guard."

I nodded. I was sure it was not just the lack of security, but also the attention I would draw if I continued to stay here, camped out in Lord Toric's bed.

He looked down at me, his body stilling as if he were listening, or maybe reading something in my face that only he could see. "I regret that we must part ways now, Maya." Raising his hand, he reached out as if to brush my cheek but pulled back before his fingers touched my skin. He turned as someone else arrived.

"My Lord." A guard stood there—Calvin. I recognized him as the one who'd stayed behind to watch over me in the ballroom.

Lord Toric went over to him, but spoke loud enough that I could hear. "She must remain under constant protection. I will not have another incident."

Calvin nodded smartly, touched his earpiece, and said a few words I couldn't hear. He stayed where he was, obviously waiting to escort Lord Toric to his meeting.

The alien Lord cast a long look at me before turning and following his guard out the door.

I couldn't imagine when Lord Toric and I might have a moment alone again, and disappointment gripped my heart as I watched his retreating back. I shook my head and touched my fingers to my lips, wondering again if I were trapped in a strange dream.

A contingent of guards and medics soon arrived. The medics pushed a gurney to the bed and helped me onto it, and then we trooped through the corridors of the palace and down to the Obligates' quarters, drawing curious stares from servants and nobles alike.

After depositing me in my quarters, the medics left with their gurney. All of the guards, but the one to remain stationed outside my door, departed as well.

I settled myself into bed, trying to focus on resting but instead alternating between fretting over the next challenge of the Tournament and replaying the heat of Lord Toric's kiss. I touched my lips again and closed my eyes but then forced my thoughts to my own survival.

I would need every bit of energy to do well in the Tournament, even under the best circumstances, but I could barely walk across the room under my own power. I sent up a prayer that Lord Toric would convince Akantha to delay the challenge, but I wasn't hopeful.

There was a soft rap at the door. "Maya, it's Iris."

"Please come in," I called.

My heart lifted at the sight of my guide's face. If I'd had the strength, I would have raced to her and wrapped my arms around her slim shoulders.

"I'm so glad to see you," I said. I blinked back unexpected tears and shook my head. "So much has happened, I don't even know where to start . . ."

She sat on the edge of the bed and placed her hand on my forearm. "Are you okay? I was told of your ordeal."

"I was drugged, and I still haven't fully recovered my strength. Lord Toric—" I faltered, unsure of what to say about what had happened between me and the alien Lord. Unsure if what I remembered had actually happened at all. "He found me, and he—he took care of me. He showed me great kindness."

I felt heat rising to my face as she tilted her head and gave me a curious look. "So I was right. He does indeed favor you in ways that extend beyond the Tournament."

I gave a short laugh. "Orion tried to tell me exactly that and I didn't believe him, but . . . perhaps there is something to what you say." I shook my head again. "But I—well, I don't really know what it all means."

I buried my face in my hands as a rush of emotion churned through my chest.

"Something like this happened once before," Iris said, her voice so soft I barely heard the words.

I dropped my hands. "What do you mean?"

"It was in Lord Alec's time, just before I arrived here on Calisto. One of the Obligates in the group just before mine. I've only heard the stories, but . . . there was a young woman that Lord Alec was deeply drawn to. But the tide of the great battles took a sudden turn in the favor of the Calistans and Lord Alec was called away. While he was gone, the Obligate was murdered. Lord Alec plunged into a terrible depression and the Calistans lost their advantage in the war."

"Was the girl's murderer ever brought to justice?" I asked.

"No." Iris gave me a long look. "Lord Toric is wise to keep you under protection."

I grimaced. "It's not going to matter much if I don't survive the next challenge. I don't know what I'm going to do. Lord Toric said he would try to convince Akantha to delay the next challenge, but she doesn't seem to have much generosity of spirit, especially toward Obligates." Fear edging on panic began to take over again. "Iris, I can barely walk."

She squeezed my arm with gentle pressure. "Try to summon calm and courage, Maya. You have something now that you didn't have before. You know that Lord Toric wants you to win. He wants *you*. He is a clever and powerful man, and if there is any way he can shift things in your favor, he will. You must keep your head about you."

I took a deep breath, recalling the way he'd looked at me. The tenderness in his touch. The passion in his kiss.

"But he is not allowed to help me win," I said. "He told me so outright."

She nodded. "Yes, that's true. But there may be things he can do that don't violate the sacred texts. If so, I'm certain he will find a way."

When I'd been selected to leave Earthenfell for Calisto I'd believed it was a fluke, a terrible turn of fate and the worst possible thing that could happen to me. But a new certainty blazed up inside me. I knew my fate was irrevocably tied to the alien Lord's.

Next in the series:
Sapient Salvation Book 2: The Awakening

For fun extras from the authors, go to CCJFbooks.com and join their insider's list!

Text **CCJFBOOKS to 24587** and you'll get text message alerts for new releases and special deals on all Jayne Faith books!

Interview with Author Jayne Faith

Question 1: What inspired you to create Maya?

Jayne Faith: I wanted to write a character who started out very innocent—sheltered and sexually inexperienced—and show how she grows and leaves innocence behind, partly out of her own desire to do so but more so because of her circumstances. Early in *The Selection*, Maya's reality and her expectations for her future get completely rocked, and she's forced away from everything she knows. We love to see what characters do when they're shoved out of their comfort zones, and that was my aim with Maya.

I chose my Maya's name very deliberately—it's a name and word that appears across many languages and cultures, sometimes with slight variations in spelling. Just a few examples: "Maia" is the Greek variation, "maya" means "love" in Nepali, Mya is a Muslim name, "Maija" is the Finnish variation of the name, "Mayu" is a Japanese name that means "truth," and "Maya" appears in Hindu mythology and means "illusion" [source: Wikipedia]. I love these various definitions that come from such disparate cultures—combined, they describe Maya as a person as well as hint at her role in the story. Symbolically, I wanted Maya to be universal, a young woman who simultaneously belongs everywhere and nowhere, and her name captures this, too.

Question 2: So many questions still remain at the end of Book 1: Who was behind Maya's abduction? Who delivered the secret volume of the sacred text to the Priestess? How close are the Calistans to their Return to Earth? What does Jeric want from Maya? Will Maya survive the next challenge? Will she and Lord Toric be able to explore their new bond under so many watchful eyes?

Will we learn any of the answers in Book 2 – *The Awakening*?

Jayne Faith: Oh yes, you'll find out the answers to at least a couple of those questions! The mystery of who was behind Maya's abduction will be a key one in *The Awakening*. And you'll definitely get more development of the relationship between Maya and Toric—with a couple of big wrenches thrown into the works, like Toric's impending responsibility to find a Calistan wife.

Question 3: Lord Toric seems to have a dark past—what can you tell us about it?

Jayne Faith: I can't help but feel for Toric because even though he's the Lord of Calisto and Earth, he hasn't had it easy in life. In *The Selection*, you got a few hints about his abduction and torture when he was a boy. He still bears deep scars from the experience, which will come into play more and more as he and Maya grow closer. You already know that Toric's brother

Jeric cruelly reminds Toric of his torture and its effects, but as the story progresses you'll learn that Jeric is not the only key person in Toric's life who harbors an unfair prejudice about Toric because of his abduction and torture.

Question 4: What's the meaning of the series name, "Sapient Salvation?"

Jayne Faith: Sapient has two meanings: "wise" and "human." I like it because it's kind of a science-fictiony word (I love science fiction!), and also for the dual meaning. The two most important characters in the story—Maya and Toric—are human in both the literal sense (they're both descended from the same human ancestors) and in the sense that they have a lot to overcome. They each possess wisdom they have yet to realize, and both of them need saving in some way. "Sapient Salvation" seemed like a catchy and meaningful series name.

Question 5: What other books have you written?

Jayne Faith: My co-author Christine Castle and I also have two futuristic adventure romances:
The Seas of Time is a sci-fi time travel romance that takes place under the ocean—with sexy tattooed mermen!
The Laws of Attraction is a futuristic space opera romance that's perfect for fans of Firefly, Star Wars (especially the Han Solo-Princess Leia romance), and Farscape.